Copyright © 2021 Isabelle Johnson

All rights reserved. No part of this publication may be reproduced, distributed, or transmitted in any form or by any means, including photocopying, recording, or other electronic or mechanical methods, without the prior written permission of the publisher, except in the case of brief quotations embodied in critical reviews and certain other noncommercial uses permitted by copyright law.

ISBN: 9798499361658 (paperback)

Any references to historical events, real people, or real places are used fictitiously. Names, characters, and places are products of the author's imagination

More by Isabelle Johnson

The Incredible Adventures of Mr. Marxadue

The Curious Shop on Dandelion Lane

Table of Contents

Author's Note 7
Dedications 11
Chapter 1. 12
Chapter 2. 24
Chapter 3 40
Chapter 4 52
Chapter 5. 63
Chapter 6 75
Chapter 7 97
Chapter 8. 116
Chapter 9. 136
Chapter 10. 146
Chapter 11. 163
Chapter 12 174

Chapter 13. 198
Chapter 14. 209
Chapter 15 222
Chapter 16. 226
Chapter 17. 234
Epilogue. 246
Acknowledgements. 248

Author's Note

I remember the exact day I started writing this story. How I came up with the idea isn't very romantic, so I think I'll keep that part to myself. But, it was a cool, peaceful day, while the world was turning upside down in the middle of a global pandemic. At the time, I was working on a dystopian novel, but with the current circumstances, my heart just wasn't in it. There were so many things happening in the world, and I needed an escape. Somewhere that was green, with a bright sun and the ocean so close you could hear it while you walked down the streets. Maybe a white cottage with an iron fence and flowers, where cats would wander in and out and butterflies made their homes. When I first got the idea for this story, it didn't mean much at the time. There wasn't much to it besides Lydia and a shop, but, a little over a year later, here we are. And now here you are, reading this for maybe the first time, and you have no idea what you're about to read. I find that somewhat odd. I know this story in and out. I know every detail, every quirk, every small, intricate word that means a thousand other things, but to anyone else it means nothing. I love that. I really do. That this story is so unique that it means something different to everyone.

I recall a conversation I had with my mom after she read it for the first time. When I asked her about the characters, the way she read them was completely opposite of how I intended. However, though I thought that it would upset me, it only made me more confident in the universality of the novel. The characters are funny and real, and no matter who you are, you can see yourself and others in their place. And, I think that's what makes a good story: when the reader forgets that they're reading. When they can open a book and instantly become one with a character and immediately connect with the others. When a reader has an instant connection to your characters, you know you've done your job.

So, as you read this, I hope you find both the good and bad in each of these characters. Though I love them all dearly, they are human. Completely and utterly human (kind of). They fall, they make mistakes, they lie and cheat, but I think that's why they mean so much to me. They're no different than I am, and it's important that we remind ourselves that we can always be getting better. We can always *be* better.

This stuck with me while I wrote this book: this idea that we can always be better. At a time in the world filled with turmoil and sadness, I wrote this story to try and bring in some light. *The Curious Shop on Dandelion Lane* is a story of love, of forgiveness, of moving forward even when all hope feels lost, and persevering under the worst of circumstances. And of course, in the end, love conquers all.

What I love about this story is all the fun little personal things I snuck in there. There's much more to it than you would think, but one of my favorite things about writing is when someone reads your story, and then you get to watch their face as you explain to them what it all really meant. I put a few easter eggs in this book, so I hope you find them.

I used to think I was writing this story for myself, but I think it's supposed to be much bigger than that. This story is yours just as much as it is mine, and that's what makes it so special. I hope you fall in love with it all just as much as I did: the magic, the characters, the adventure, and all of the quirks in-between. This story is so important to me for so many reasons, and I am so grateful for every word I was privileged to write. I hope you find as much joy in this as I do, and I hope that it makes your day a little bit better. Isn't that all we can do? Just try to make the world a little bit better?

I think that's the point. Though we fall and stumble and mess up so many times, I think we're all supposed to try and make the world a better place, no matter how significant or miniscule. And, just like the characters in this novel, we will fail. We will fail miserably, and hurt those around us and just make a huge mess of everything. But, part of making the world better is admitting our faults, and recognizing that we are human first, no matter what else happens to us.

And, just as we are human, we are the only ones who can bring some good into this place. So go read, go create, go explore, and go help someone who needs it. You'll be helping yourself just as much as you're helping them.

Before you move on and begin reading, I would just like to offer you my thanks. I cannot begin to describe how excited and grateful I am that you decided to pick up this book, and I truly hope it impacts you as grandly as it did me. I wish you the best on your adventures, and I offer you all of my sincerest gratitude.

>With all of my love,
>
>Isabelle Johnson

To Mom and Dad

1

Lydia wandered down the busy streets of Brightmeadow on the finest of Sunday afternoons. Though the sun hung at its peak and beat down on the busy streets, the ladies all donned their nicest coats, and the gentlemen their hats. People shuffled in and out of the shops lining the sides of the wide road. Lydia waited patiently for the train trolley to slide through the middle of the street and part the crowds, but it still had yet to arrive. She had no real reason to ride the trolley in the first place. It didn't take her anywhere she needed to go. She only did it for fun, for there was not much else for her to do.

"Almost two o'clock," she thought to herself, "And I suppose it shall be late once more."

So, she sat herself on the black iron bench in front of Mrs. Daisy's Sewing Shop and placed her head in her hands lazily. As the people strolled by, she acted out each of their conversations in her head (and uttered them quietly aloud).

Mrs. Candy strutted along in a busy pink dress with her latest suitor attached on her arm. He had been the sixth (or was it seventh?) of the last two months, and Lydia was all too sure his time was nearly up. The last suitor, Davey (or was it Michael?), cried for days over this frivolous tramp. No one ever saw the men again after Mrs. Candy was done with them. Some say they ran away in heartbreak, and others say they never left their houses again. Over *this* woman! Lydia had no kind words to say to her or about her, and that was that. Much like the other wealthy and conceited families of Brightmeadow, Mrs. Candy's money and men seemed to define her.

"Oh dear, Mr. Jacobs," Lydia hummed to herself in a nasally, mocking tone, "I'm sure I shall be bored of you soon. Now run along and go fetch me some truffles. I'm positively wasting away under these garments."

"Good afternoon, Miss Mayler. Fine weather today isn't it?" Lydia tilted her head at Cedric, whose face was nearly hidden behind the load of things he carried in his arms. Cedric was the apprentice to the old, crabby shoemaker in town, Mr. Barley. Though Cedric and Lydia were dear friends, she often thought he smiled all too much at the wrong times, for most of the time he could think of nothing reasonable to smile about other than the outright action of doing so. Admittedly, she admired his joy, but she couldn't help giggling as she watched him struggle to hold all of Mr. Barley's boxes and tools while being bustled around between people.

"You say the weather is just right everyday," Lydia said matter-of-factly, though the playful tone in her voice did not go unnoticed by Cedric.

"Well, that's because it *is* every day."

"To you, maybe." Lydia brushed the short curls from her face, her bangs still stuck lightly to the perspiration beading on her forehead.

"Hurry along now, Cedric. Don't hold up the waiting line," Mr. Barley croaked.

Cedric sighed with a hint of optimism. "Cheers for now."

With a wave of her hand goodbye, Cedric hurried along beside Mr. Barley, stumbling and grabbing things falling from his hands.

Lydia observed the people for a few minutes longer, then checked the clock on the square once more.

"Two sixteen. I suppose the trolley is altogether much too busy for me," she sighed. "Though I wish it wasn't so hot. Perhaps I would enjoy the day as Cedric does."

Lydia often talked to herself. She could think of no one better to converse with, and usually she spoke the sincerest advice.

She fixed her creme colored hat and brushed the dust off her green flowered dress. Her mother didn't expect her home until six o'clock at the latest, and Lydia figured she ought to make some use of the day.

Normally, she would trail up and down Magnolia Street and peek in and out of shops to say hello to familiar faces, but today, the sun cooked the marketplace like a fried egg, and Lydia could not stand the stuffiness of the crowd. As quickly as she could navigate through the people, she marched herself in the opposite way of the crowds to the very end of the street and turned the corner to the right. There were far less people down this way (because the trolleyman always refused to run his trolley down this street) and the shop-covers shaded the ends of the sidewalk.

In her years, she could think of only a handful of times she explored this route of the marketplace. Dandelion Lane, it was called. The stores were bland and dull (Mr. Duncan's Skin Ointments was truly ghastly), and Lydia never ran into any fellow acquaintances. Either straight down Magnolia Street or make a left turn on Statesville Lane to go home.

Lydia wandered along the edge of shops, smelling perfumes and running her hands through woven tapestries and feathered jackets. She never understood feathered jackets. Wouldn't they itch too much? The idea disturbed her, and she promised herself to never wear one, even if her mother insisted. And she would most certainly insist. As a girl with a fond interest in sewing, Lydia often found herself harboring *very* strong opinions about any sort of fashion she saw. Ladies' dresses and gowns, men's coats, and whether or not someone was wearing the right kind of hat for his or her outfit.

Strolling along, she counted the signs and thought to herself which shop might be the most interesting to explore. After all, she rarely came down this street, and she figured at least *one* business would be worth her time. Then again, she *did* have quite a while until she was expected home. Why rush?

Doyle Tapestries, Fitzgerald's Handmade Suit Coats, Custom Hats for Gentleman, the list went on. None struck the interest of Lydia enough to pause her day to further inquire. At last, she reached the end of the street, which was marked by grandiose flower arrangements and an intricate black iron fence.

She sighed. "What a chore of a day." She stuck her hands in her pockets and noticed the forgotten slip of paper she carried: a shopping list from her mother, one of which she had dismissed entirely. "Better than doing nothing, I suppose."

So, back down Magnolia Street she traveled. The crowd had thinned slightly, making it much easier to push through and enter the stores. First, she stopped by and purchased tea and biscuits from Mrs. Edmonson, then fabric thread from Mrs. Maria. Sometimes, Mrs. Maria would sneak Lydia a few small slips of leftover fabric, knowing the particular interest Lydia shared with her when it came to sewing.

The sun seemed to grow hotter every minute, but Lydia complied with her mother's wishes and paid the ladies their money in exchange for small boxes with assortments of teas and fabrics. Now, the clock on the street-pole read two-eighteen, barely putting a dent in her remaining free time. Groaning, she wandered down the street with a bored expression in search of anything to give her some sense of adventure.

She had no work to do today. That was a rare occurrence, for it seemed that the worst of the house-hold chores always fell to Lydia: doing the dirtiest laundry, tidying up after a particularly messy evening, cleaning the dishes. . .the list continued on. Now, though, Lydia wasn't sure if she preferred the heat over the boring chores. What good is time with no practical way to spend it?

Lydia found herself along a familiar trail of the woods a good distance from Magnolia Street. The trees shaded the dirt path and sweet air drifted along the breeze. This trail led to Dahlia Road, the neighborhood by the sea where the rich people of Brightmeadow lived. Lydia's family wasn't wealthy, but they were well-off enough to live comfortably. She never really sought out wealth like others around town did. If anything, she would be merely content impressing them with her success without the addition of money to help her. Lydia scolded herself silently, knowing that there wasn't any need to impress them in the first place. Though, she thought, it *would* feel nice to be seen.

She smelled the same flowers as she always did and ran her hands along the bark on the trees. The same old thing, day after day. Would it ever change?

***

Lydia arrived home about an hour and a half later. She opened the white gate to her front yard, which bloomed with an assortment of flowers. Peonies, chrysanthemums, lilies, and all sorts of roses were just a few of the blossoms that covered the garden's every inch. Ivy ran along the white cottage walls and along the brick chimney. The stones on the pathway had moss speckling the edges and daffodils sprouting from the cracks and crevices in-between. Lydia enjoyed skipping and jumping from one to the other, for if she fell, she would fall among a blanket of petals.

She balanced the box on her hip and opened the door to the scent of fresh bread and fruit. A blurry figure hurried to greet her and yapped and jumped at her feet. Lydia giggled and patted Rosie's head; a small chihuahua with ginger fur and all too much of an attitude. Mrs. Mayler often enjoyed dressing Rosie in cute little clothes that one *should* put on an infant, but it was no secret that the rest of the household found the outfits rather amusing. Today, Rosie leapt about in a pink dress with a white bonnet. Trudy, the cat that wandered in and out as she pleased, glared at Rosie with a haughty eye, then pranced outside through the cracked open door.

"I'm home, everyone," Lydia called, bringing the box to her mother, who was kneading a large ball of dough on her wooden table. "I brought your things."

"Thank you, dear. Just set them over there." Mrs. Mayler pointed over to the countertop. Lydia sat the box down and took a chair across from her mother and watched her work the thick dough. "Fruit?"

Lydia nodded, and made herself a bowl, then poured honey over top of it.

"Is father still at the shop?" Lydia asked. Her mother nodded, still concerned with kneading the dough beneath her hands. Rosie pawed and begged for a piece of Lydia's fruit underneath the table. When Mrs. Mayler wasn't looking, Lydia snuck Rosie a small blueberry.

"He'll be back soon. Why do you ask?"

"I fear for the safety of his wedding ring. You'll never guess who's found herself a new gentleman," Lydia said with a smirk.

Mrs. Mayler scowled and punched the dough. "I wish I didn't instantly know who you were speaking of. That frightful woman, Mrs. Candy. . .it's so unkind of me, the thoughts I think about her!"

"Well, I'm sure you're not the only one." Lydia popped a strawberry in her mouth. "Let's just hope she never comes after poor old Henry."

"What about me?" The little pest of a boy wandered in with dirty overalls and mud on his face—Henry, the younger brother of Lydia, and the troublemaker of the family. He was a kind boy, yet *so* mischievous.

"Henry! What have you done to your clothes?" Mrs. Mayler exclaimed, running over with a rag and wiping down his face. He tried to squirm away, but his mother's grip was too strong.

"I was just *playing*."

"Whatever am I going to do with you. . ." the lady muttered. "Sit down and eat your fruit."

Henry sighed dramatically, but complied, shoving the blueberries into his mouth with big gulps. He always knew just how to get under Lydia's skin, and by the look on his face, Lydia knew he was up to no good. Next thing she knew, Henry started to chuck his blueberries across the table straight for Lydia's face.

"Henry, stop it!" Lydia exclaimed, tossing a blueberry right back, which hit him in the eye. Henry gasped, then covered his face and began to cry loudly. "Oh, quiet, you. You're *fine*."

"Lydia, what have you done to your brother?" Mrs. Mayler sighed.

"I haven't done a single thing. He's just a baby."

"Am not!" he cried.

"Lydia! Go outside and leave your brother alone."

"Are you serious? I didn't even do anything!" Lydia protested.

"*Go*, Lydia."

Lydia *humphed*, then stomped out of the room and into her back yard, which was just as infested with vines and flowers as the front. She groaned and kicked at the weeds growing at the bottom of the metal fence. Bumblebees fled from her wrath, as did the birds that nested in the many birdhouses around the yard. A single butterfly fluttered down from the apple tree that shaded Lydia's head and landed on her knee.

"I suppose you're the only one who isn't angry with me."

The butterfly fidgeted as Lydia ushered it onto her finger. Its purple and blue wings flapped lazily. She smiled, observing the creature and every one of its colors.

"How lucky you are to be free to go anywhere you please."

The butterfly said nothing, of course, for it was unable to speak. How silly of Lydia to believe such a creature could respond. Perhaps she'd be talking to *frogs* next. Then, just as the wind does, the butterfly flew away on the breeze and disappeared from sight.

"Once again, I find myself alone."

The chirping of birds stopped at the sound of a loud snapping noise, making them flutter away and up into the sky.

"Hello?" Lydia called, only earning a groan as a response. She hurried to the edge of the metal fence and looked beyond the grass and trees, watching as Cedric lay on the ground in a sad sort of way. He looked up at the branches and shook his fist.

"Curse you, you worthless old tree!"

"Cedric, what on earth are you doing down there?" Lydia asked from her fence, giggling at the frustrated look on his face. He sighed, then dragged himself over to Lydia with a dejected pout. "Has Mr. Barley finally relieved you from his hostage?"

Cedric laughed sarcastically then, after thinking about it, nodded.

"I figured. What were you doing laying over there in the dirt?"

"I thought I could climb that tree right there, but the branches had other plans."

"How far did you make it?" Lydia asked.

"I believe I counted ten branches high."

Lydia thought for a moment. "I bet I could make it to fifteen."

Cedric scoffed. "Is that a challenge?"

"Of course. Now, hold my hat."

Lydia climbed over the fence, which wasn't very difficult. Climbing this tree, however, was a different story. Cedric took her hat and walked with her to the large oak towering over the other plants. Lydia tied her hair back and took a deep breath.

"Well, here I go," Lydia said, then quickly added, "And please don't tell my mother."

The first few branches were the most difficult, but the farther up Lydia climbed, the more grip she got.

"Six, seven. . .eight. . ."

The ninth branch was a bit of a reach, but with a little push she made it, then hoisted her legs up and caught the tenth branch.

"Cedric! I'm at the tenth!" She shouted down. He returned a thumbs up.

She continued to climb, almost falling at the twelfth branch, but managed to hang on tight enough to regain her balance.

"Fifteen, Cedric!"

He cheered, but she wasn't ready to climb down quite yet. Her arms moved higher, hoisting her body towards the top. She hadn't yet thought how she would make it down, but it didn't matter at the time. All she could think to do was keep going, find her way to the top of the tree, and be the tallest and most majestic thing this bleak town would ever see.

Lydia was so close to the top by now, she could see the clouds peeking through the leaves. With just a few more branches, her head peeked over the leaves and branches to reveal the sky. All around her she could see for miles. On one side, she saw Magnolia Street and the bundles of people blurring by. On the other, she saw all the way down her street,

Statesville, which was lined with many magnificent trees. A bird perched on the branch next to her, flying gracefully around her head.

"Cedric! Look up here!" She shouted. Cedric ran along the length of the yard to see up at the top of the tree. He jumped in the air when he noticed Lydia waving from the very top. He began to shout something back, but Lydia couldn't quite make out his words. She pointed to her ears and shook her head.

"I can't hear you!"

Cedric must not have noticed, as he continued to run in circles and shout up at her. Lydia laughed, then studied the town as a butterfly or bird would. The street intersection was just as she knew it to be. There were four roads, each stretching in a wide pathway with an array of shops, customers, and open markets: Magnolia Street to her east, Dandelion to her north, Statesville to her south, and Crestview to her west. Brightmeadow was much larger than she anticipated, and she even noticed the ends of each road were not actually the ends of the street. When she looked down Dandelion Lane, it stretched farther than she remembered. Peering closer, in the far corner a sign appeared that she hadn't ever noticed before. She couldn't read it from all the way up in the tree, but it was green and small. It couldn't be Doyle Tapestries or Fitzgerald's Home-Made Suits—their signs were much larger and intricate, and she could make out those from the tree. It was as if the store was hiding amidst the crowd like it didn't want to be seen. But, in her curiosity, Lydia saw it. And, it would do well to add that Lydia often noticed things that didn't want to be seen.

The sun relentlessly beat down on the tree, heating Lydia along with it. Sweat formed at her brow and stained her dress.

"What a shame. It's beautiful up here," she said out loud to herself before she decided to climb back down. She looked down at the array of branches and suddenly realized that climbing *up* the tree wasn't the difficult part.

"Now. . .how on earth will I make it down?"

2

Later that night, the Mayler family all sat down together for dinner. Mr. Mayler had surprised them each with a pastry to go along with Mrs. Mayler's meal. Henry was incredibly pleased with this and refused most of his vegetables in exchange for the chocolate muffin.

"Eat your food, Henry. You need to grow up big and strong." Mr. Mayler ruffled Henry's already messy hair into a funny looking curl. Henry shook his hand away and laughed.

Lydia could hear her family speaking, but none of it quite registered to her. She was stuck much too far back in her thoughts and imagination. No matter how hard she tried, she couldn't lose the image of that strange, hidden shop. Sure, she hadn't explored Dandelion Lane often, but Lydia certainly believed she would have realized that place before. Perhaps it was just her boredom creating fantasies?

"A very odd man came into the shop today," Mr. Mayler said with a shake of the head, "Felt bad for him. All skinny and quiet and such. Couldn't see his face, but he was polite."

"You don't suppose it was—" She made a knowing face to her husband.

"Who? Mr. Miller?" He shrugged and bit into a tomato. "What does it matter? I've never met the bloke."

This wasn't the first time Lydia heard the name of a Mr. Miller uttered. Her mother often made her skepticism known. "Well, people talk, you know. Ms. Maria heard he was a thief on the run and he stays in Brightmeadow as a quiet protection from his past convictions."

He grunted, which wasn't a reply good enough for his wife.

"And Mrs. Fisher heard he was a criminal on the run for—well, she didn't really know what."

"Lovely, dear." He wasn't paying attention.

"And—I'm sure you'll get a kick out of this—Mr. Fitzgerald once heard he swindled a load of people out of their money and now he goes from town to town trying to do the same. No *wonder* he has no business in that strange old shop of his. Everyone's terrified! Then again, half the people in Brightmeadow don't even know he has his own shop, let alone know where it is. Only the shop owners are aware. Competition, you know, but ask any pedestrian and they'd be clueless! How funny is that?"

Mr. Mayler glanced up from his paper to meet expectant eyes from Mrs. Mayler. Obviously, he had no idea how to respond, as he wasn't paying her mind, so he subtly looked to Lydia for help. She nodded to signal a positive response.

"Yes, dear, you're just right. Right as always, of course."

Lydia gave a sly thumbs up to her relieved father. Mrs. Mayler, quite pleased with the response, said nothing else about the matter and enjoyed her strawberry muffin.

* * *

Mr. Mayler volunteered to work the shop for the day, leaving plenty of free time for Lydia (once she finished her own responsibilities). She had her plans to examine the unknown shop, of course, but she had to make sure she finished her chores perfectly as not to raise questions about her plans from her mother. So, after watering the herbs, cleaning the leftover dishes, and hanging up the laundry (mostly just dirty pairs of Henry's shirts and socks), Lydia was at last free to roam. She kissed her mother's cheek goodbye and tugged gently on Henry's hair. Rosie licked her hand once as she made her way through the flowery drive.

As usual for a day like this, the streets were crowded with people and conversations, which were most likely incredibly boring. Sometimes, Lydia would eavesdrop for fun and come to her own conclusions about the topic at hand. Cedric would join in sometimes too, that is, when he was around. He worked much more than Lydia did, but that was mostly because Mr. Barley himself was an old shoe.

Just as she expected, Dandelion Lane was nearly empty in comparison to Magnolia Street. She peeked in the windows of shops just for fun, but she really wasn't interested. Just stalling, and doing her best to not look too suspicious. She didn't look suspicious in the first place, but the whole idea of sneaking around in secret was rather exciting, and she wanted to play it up in her mind.

She reached the end of the lane and, just like yesterday, there wasn't anything unusual or unseen to her. Just the empty green sign and a dusty window. It looked like an empty store, waiting for a new owner to arrive.

Lydia sighed, and figured she just might have to return home early due to a failed adventure, when a gleam caught her eye. She examined it closer, and saw it was not in fact a result of a beaming sun, but rather a strange, glowing trinket in a dusty old shop window. So dusty, in fact, you could hardly see through it. The green sign she recognized from the tree swayed gently in the wind. Faded, golden trimmed red letters on the sign read:

Mr. Miller's Shop of Antiques and Antiquities

Lydia recalled hearing her mother mutter secretly to her father about this shop. Last night wasn't the *only* time her parents whispered about this place. It was always complaints about business competition, and how it wasn't even fair a new shop would appear from nowhere, and it was rather strange no one seemed to know who the owner was. Under his breath, her father agreed it was indeed a very strange place. No place fit for a young girl like Lydia, of course. She had never stumbled across the shop and for many years, she believed it to be a fairy tale. It was something of an urban legend in Brightmeadow. Only among the shop owners, though. They would whisper curiously about it, as if it were a strange creature lurking in the shadows. Lydia was a smart girl and knew to stay out of trouble, but sometimes she wondered what would happen if she went against her parent's wishes and sought her own adventures. They warned her to stay away and to not satisfy her curiosity, but standing in front of that dusty old window, Lydia knew she had to reveal the secrets that called to her within. It was just a store, she thought. How could that possibly do her any harm? Besides, it wasn't even three o'clock yet, and her mother would never even have to know. She would walk in, look around for a few minutes, then walk right back out. No harm done.

She looked down the street, then behind her, just to make sure no one was watching. *Why would it matter if someone was watching?* she thought to herself, but she soon resolved to the idea that the secrecy of the whole situation made it so much more exhilarating.

The brass doorknob shivered under Lydia's hand, beckoning for her to turn it ever so slightly to the left to free the dust collecting at the hinge of the door. Just a bit further. . .

"Lydia Mayler? Is that you, darling?"

And in an instant, Lydia yanked her hand away from the brass as if it had scalded her and jumped away from the door. Mrs. Fisher, a customer of Lydia's mother, smiled warmly and clasped her hands together.

"Good afternoon, Mrs. Fisher. A pleasure as always," Lydia said kindly, though she was rather irritated to be interrupted.

"Indeed it is. Say, would you mind telling your mother I have an order inquiry for her? Rather grand this one is, and I just know she gets so busy during this time of the year."

Mrs. Mayler was a florist, and a rather gifted one at that. In fact, her flowers and arrangements were so lovely and admirable, she had put all the other florists out of business. Though she told everyone she felt deeply guilty and sorry, the large sum of money she made proved otherwise and quickly made up for any apologetic feelings Mrs. Mayler might have felt. Sometimes, she had Lydia work the shop while she tended to her flowers, but most often Lydia was out and about doing whatever business she felt like during the day. Mrs. Fisher had been one of the first customers to inquire about the Mayler's services, and it seemed she always had a grandiose need for banquets and elaborate parties: parties filled with the most sophisticated of people, according to *her* standards. And though Mrs. Mayler was a classy woman and provided Mrs. Fisher with the best of services, the Maylers hadn't *once* received a fancy invitation to a party carefully formulated by Mrs. Fisher. She was a mostly polite lady, but Lydia hadn't ever thought of her as a friend, nor of someone she would choose to converse with. You see, Mrs. Fisher was one of those *wealthy* ladies who perched in her large, fancy house on Dahlia Road. She was altogether *much* to good for people like Lydia in her opinion. Or so she made Lydia feel.

"Of course, ma'am. I'll see to it she receives this as quickly as I can manage."

Mrs. Fisher dug through her expensive purse with her white gloves, rummaging around for a candy to pop into her dry mouth. Lydia squinted her brow at her thick, lacy clothing, which must have been two degrees away from causing this woman a heatstroke.

"Thank you, dear. And tell your father I said to behave!"

And, just as the filthy rich always do, Mrs. Fisher tried to milk a joke out of the very little knowledge she had of the family she asked service from. Lydia recalled the one and only time Mrs. Fisher ever spoke to her father, but knowing a sum of cash greater than any other order would soon roll in, Lydia faked a smile.

"I certainly will."

The frilly lady hurried off with a skip in her step, fanning herself with an expensive fan made of the finest silk and lace. Lydia glanced down at her brown boots and thin dress that reached the middle of her shins and wondered what it would be like to dress as handsomely as women like Mrs. Fisher—to disregard the heat or the cold, and don the most expensive silks and fabrics embroidered with jewels and intricate patterns. To throw parties with the most sophisticated people, most of whom you weren't even familiar with, you were just aware they were *almost* as rich as you. To be able to buy any sort of trinket or crumpet your heart desired for the evening, and then not even finish it because you ended up purchasing a fair amount that was much too large for your own appetite.

What a wasteful life! Lydia thought, but still retained that dearest memory in the back of her mind. Turning back to the dusty store to follow through with her business, she now saw that the light inside the window had dimmed, turning the store dark and blank. A slip of paper hung on the door that Lydia swore hadn't been there before.

Sincerest apologies; Mr. Miller's Shop is closed for the day.

Lydia pouted and tried to see through the old window, but it was no use. She tried to knock on the door to receive some sort of response, but once again nothing.

"Well! I suppose I haven't anything to do besides return home hours early!" She called, as if to beckon a response out of the old shop. Only silence. Defeated, she *humphed* and made her way back down to Magnolia Street, not even noticing the flicker of movement behind the window.

***

Mrs. Mayler had promised Henry last week that they would spend the day picking fresh apples from the tree and baking pies together. Lydia knew how important it was to both of them, so she willingly volunteered to host the shop for the day. Mr. Mayler had to travel to the next town over to purchase a special soil fertilizer, an item that was not exclusively sold at Brightmeadow. So, Lydia and her mother ate breakfast together with each other's company. They spoke of people and the town, both good and bad, yet they always seemed to come to the same conclusion about people. Lydia hoped that would apply to her next question.

"Mum?"

Mrs. Mayler hummed in response and sipped her tea.

"Do you—just—out of total curiosity—know anything about that shop at the edge of Dandelion Lane?"

Her eyes grew wide and once as she sat her tea cup down calmly. "Why do you ask?"

"Curious," she said a bit too quickly, "Just a bit curious."

"It's been there for quite a while," she replied, "I'm not really sure how long. Mr. Miller is the man that runs it. I think. No one's met him. Everyone seems to think they know him, though. Oh, I've heard it all. A thief, a man on the run, a criminal with a good heart, a criminal with a bad heart, I've told you all that before. . .well, I just believe he's a bit of a stranger. Never shows his face. I know for a fact no one would be able to recognize him if they did happen to see him."

Lydia thought about this. "Why does everyone want to believe they know him, then?"

"Because people hate those they don't understand."

Lydia nodded to herself. She understood what she meant, but she wished it weren't true. It made her the slightest bit guilty. Here she was, confused by others judging a man they deem strange, when she herself cast stones at women like Mrs. Candy. Well, that was different, she thought. *Everyone* knew Mrs. Candy. Some people a bit more *intimately*. It seemed that no one ever *really* knew who this Mr. Miller was.

"Well, maybe one day Mrs. Candy will snag him from right under our noses."

Mrs. Mayler laughed and shook her head. "Oh, Lydia. I *fear* for that man's heart."

* * *

For an early Tuesday morning, it was much too hot already. The whole town awaited the return of rainfall, for the humidity and heat caused many a lady to faint in their flowery gowns and drizzle their fine makeup. Lydia clicked her shop keys in the door and creaked open to the smell of honey and soft petals. The flowers lasted for about three days until the withering ensued. Sometimes, if lucky, even four. By then, though, the Maylers usually had new arrangements ready.

For the next few hours, Lydia helped each customer with as much enthusiasm as she could muster, but it was not much. Most of the shops closed at five o'clock, but the Mayler's Flower Shop usually closed around four-thirty. That was mostly so the family would have time to pick Henry up from school, but in the summer days it wasn't as necessary. There was no use to change it, though. Around four-fifteen is when most of the people and crowds dissolved anyway.

At long last, Lydia finished up her last bouquet and ushered the satisfied customer out. Almost all the flowers were gone, which meant tomorrow would be an early gathering morning. Sighing, she cleaned up the remnants of petals and dirty footprints, then locked the doors and ruffled her hair out of its neatness. There wasn't much else to do, so Lydia entered Mr. Barley's shoe shop to converse with Cedric about an inquiry that still had not left her mind.

Cedric polished a shoe on a stool behind the counter, hardly taking notice of Lydia's entrance. On her way, she had stopped to purchase two tomato and lettuce sandwiches—one for each of them. She placed the sandwich wrapped in light cloth in front of Cedric and rang the little silver bell on the counter. He gasped lowly, startled by the sudden noise.

"Lydia! I didn't see you there."

"I know."

He smiled and sat the shoe down beside him. "I guess I owe you the next lunch, don't I?"

Lydia smirked. "If you suppose yourself to be a gentleman."

"We'll see."

For the next fifteen minutes they shared stories of difficult customers and ridiculous orders, laughing at the stupidity of it all. Cedric and Lydia had been friends for years, and it was no secret they both knew they didn't fit in with the other children their age. The eighteen year olds in Brightmeadow had a much different vision for their lives than Lydia and Cedric did, but that's what made them so unmistakably special. Lydia's thoughts hung in the back of her mind for the entire conversation, until at last she was able to have the courage to speak up.

"Cedric, may I ask you something?"

As if he were waiting for this moment for years, he placed his head in his hands and nodded eagerly for Lydia to continue.

"Do you know anything about Mr. Miller?"

Cedric's eyes fell slightly, as if he were disappointed by the question. He sighed, then looked away. "Mr. Miller from the port?"

"No, the one with the shop the next street over."

"I'm afraid I don't. Why do you ask?"

Lydia shrugged and fiddled with some of the loose fabric pieces on the table. "I'm not quite sure. I passed by his shop and it just seemed. . .so interesting." Lydia shrugged away the thought after she noticed the look on Cedric's face. "I'm probably just being dramatic, aren't I?"

Cedric pursed his lips. "I don't mean to judge harshly, but I wouldn't go and explore his shop any further if I were you."

"Why's that?"

"Well, you know, I've heard Mr. Barley talk. Says he's a thief and he stole away some of the most precious artifacts from his hometown."

"And you *don't* want me to explore it?"

"No, that's not what I meant," Cedric replied. "All I'm saying is that you need to be careful. No one here has ever even *seen* Mr. Miller. For all we know, he could be a ghost."

"Don't be ridiculous, Cedric."

"I am *not* being ridiculous. I am merely taking a precaution for your safety." Cedric turned his nose up in the air, then continued polishing the leather on a freshly made shoe.

"I appreciate the concern, but I don't think we should act as if we know a man that we haven't ever seen."

"I've heard he is quite strange, indeed."

"And yet you also have heard he might be a ghost!" Lydia exclaimed in frustration. "Honestly, I'm so tired of this place! It's this thief this, and this ghost that! No one ever longs for anything more than a four street intersection and pointless gossip about a lonely man running a simple shop!"

The customers wandering about all paused and watched Lydia strangely. Cedric found no words to respond. Annoyed, Lydia gathered up her things and stormed out of the shop and towards the end of Dandelion Lane. She practically sprinted to the green sign hanging above the dusty shop window, relieved to see there was no *closed* notice on the door. She reached her hand out and moved the door handle, but it didn't budge.

"Locked?"

She tried once more, this time tugging on it as if that would make things any better. Throwing her hands down, she growled and shouted at the seemingly vacant windows.

"Why do you shut someone out who only dreams of helping you?"

The clouds above replied with a rumble of thunder. Lydia felt the first few cold drops sprinkle on her arms. In an instant, the rain picked up, and suddenly a downpour ensued. Once again, Lydia tried to jiggle the door open to escape the monsoon, but it was still locked.

"Really? You won't even help me to escape the rain?"

No response.

"Fine then! Have it your way! I'll just walk home in the downpour!"

And that's exactly what she did.

＊ ＊ ＊

Lydia arrived home absolutely soaked from head to toe. Mud formed on the bottom of her shoes and splashed on the back of her legs. Her hat shielded her face, but only in the slightest bit, for now the fabric was soggy and dripping with water. Lydia kicked off her boots under the small pavilion on her front door and left her hat right beside them. She made her way to the washroom, careful not to drip too much water on the floors. She grabbed a towel resting in the basket and dried herself from head to foot. The rainwater only made her curls frizz wildly. Water dripped from the edges onto the floor and pooled around her. Eventually, she gave up trying to tame the frizz and left her wet clothes hanging on the edge of the door. Her nightgown, which was dry and warm from the earlier sun, was a nice change from the freezing, soaked clothes.

"Darling, you look ghastly!" Mrs. Mayler exclaimed when Lydia slumped into a chair across from her knitting mother. "Caught in the rain?"

Lydia groaned, then left just as quickly as she entered, not wanting to be under the criticism of her mother. She sulked alone into her room and threw herself on the frilly, ruffled sheets of her bed.

Why could she not just get into that shop? Could it really be that Mr. Miller locked out the whole world for a reason? All she wanted to do was look around, just to say she did it and prove everyone in town wrong. People can be different and still be people. Did this inherent desire to fully know who Mr. Miller was stem from the fact that people in town also regarded *her* as unusual and odd, labeling her as some girl with her head in the clouds? Maybe it was, but what did it matter? Lydia would rather be in the clouds than stuck in the mud.

That night she had marvelous dreams about the possibilities behind those dusty windows. When she woke, she could not remember what those possibilities were, but when she caught a glimpse of a butterfly or a flowery pastry, a flicker of some sort of forgotten memory passed through her mind.

Mr. Mayler was working the shop today, which meant that Lydia was expected to run errands for her mother. Henry had to go and get a new shirt because he ruined one of his three with copious amounts of mud, so Mrs. Mayler gave Lydia another shopping list and a small bag of coins—just enough to purchase all she needed.

It seemed as if everyday Lydia did the same thing. She wore the same thing, visited the same stores, and talked to all the same people. She didn't mind helping her mother, but the whole strict cycle her life was built around was more boring than Mr. Barley's idea of a good time. And *that*, according to Cedric, consisted of him watching the ocean for hours on end and drinking exactly three and a half bottles of rum.

So, Lydia set out once more as she always did, in and out of the shops she had grown up with. First, to the bake shop to buy flour. Second, dairy products. Third, a new tea kettle (Henry accidentally knocked theirs over the previous night).

By the time Lydia acquired all of her items, it was only three o'clock, and she had a few leftover coins in the bag. She treated herself to a mini pie from the bakery on the corner and watched people on the street to make the time go by. She thought to herself a lot during this time about many things, most of which she didn't not fully understand, nor did she understand why she thought about them.

"Maybe the trolley will stop by," Lydia thought to herself hopefully as she sat on the same iron bench as usual. However, it did not surprise her when the trolley did not, in fact, stop by. Four o'clock. Every other hour it *should* stop, but that was never the case. "Oh, well. Walking will do the job."

She gathered up her things and began to make her way home. The heat had subsided (to her delight), and now it was only a warm, humid day. To her surprise, though, it was quite busy in the street for four o'clock in the afternoon, and she had to take special care to be mindful of the people around her.

While her head was down and counting the extra money in her bag, she happened to bump rather harshly into a man walking opposite of her. He dropped his belongings, which then sprawled along the road.

"Oh, dear, I'm terribly sorry, sir," Lydia exclaimed, hurrying to catch all of the runaway items. A ball of yarn, two loaves of bread, some cheese wrapped in light fabric, and a bundle of teas. "Here, I can get those for you."

Lydia retrieved the items and placed them delicately back inside of his basket. A cloak covered his face, but even still, Lydia was sure she had never met this man before, which was unusual considering who her mother was and how often she walked these streets. He was much taller than her, and rather skinny. He had a few silver rings on his hands, one of which stood out brightly on his right hand with a green gemstone, but it was tarnished and slightly rusted along the edges. His face was downcast, as if he expected her to be rude and unforgiving, which Lydia noticed.

"Sorry again, sir. I wasn't paying attention." He didn't respond. "Please forgive me."

He flinched, as if surprised by her words, but said nothing. He nodded, then gathered up his things and left, handing her a golden coin. Lydia gasped with excitement and turned to thank him, but he had already disappeared into the crowd.

"Well, thank you anyways!" She called still, just in case he might hear.

That night, Lydia lay awake with her thoughts as the gold coin weighed heavy against her pillow.

3

This morning, Lydia had to work, but she didn't mind. It gave her time to think to herself, which she appreciated because sometimes she occupied herself too much to be able to think. She liked thinking a lot, even if she didn't always know what exactly was on her mind. Her mind was a funny place, often twirling with random, incoherent thoughts that made perfect sense to her alone. If anyone else could hear some of the things that flicked in and out of that strange brain, most would fear for her health. Lydia didn't mind this thought, though. She often felt that being a thinker was a great compliment.

After noon, her mother came and took over the shop, so Lydia left and picked up some lunch from the bakery a few stores down. She passed by Mr. Barley's to see if Cedric was free to accompany her, but he was practically drowning in customers, so Lydia figured it best to leave him be.

She enjoyed her tomato sandwich on the same iron bench as usual, as she kept watch for the trolley. Time must have flown by much faster than she had thought, because the church bells rang out twice. She glanced down the street.

"What a surprise. . .no trolley."

Tossing the wrappings in a nearby trash can, she continued her pointless walk until she ended up right outside of the strange shop at the end of Dandelion Lane once more. She didn't remember walking this far or long, but it hardly occurred to her to be anything but curious. She tilted her head slightly, then *humphed* with an annoyed glare.

"I doubt this will work, but I suppose I might as well try anyway."

She moved forward and rested her hand on the brass doorknob and twisted it with no expectations. Much to her surprise though, she heard a soft *click*, and the door gave way. She stopped dead in her tracks, suddenly unsure if she should enter or not.

One look to the left, one look to the right, then one step forward.

Lydia stepped into the shop, coughing at the heaps of dust and strong antique smell. The light was dim, but enough sunlight shone through so every object on the cluttered shelves were visible through the dust. And oh, what a clutter!

"Hello?" She called.

No response.

Trinkets piled the shelves so tightly, they almost tipped over the shelves. Antiques and other strange possessions lined the floor pathways and leaned against the walls haphazardly: tea kettles, books, old tools, strange clocks, jars filled with old jams, faded globes, and so many more things from days past. On one of the shelves, a ceramic ballerina with a light pink tutu balanced on a glass stand. She was very pretty, and her little glass hair swooped back around her face into a perfect, shiny bun.

"What a beauty," Lydia said to herself.

Old, frayed dresses hung loosely from metal body stencils, captivating Lydia's attention. The fabric was so simple, yet so elegant: long and thin with frilly creme sleeves and a flowery corset. Lydia trailed her hands along the seams and tilted her head. Though her mother expected her to be a florist one day, Lydia often dreamed of sewing the most elegant dresses. She had yet to sell her many designs, but she hoped to one day find the courage (and, hopefully, the opportunity).

Lydia wandered about the creaky wooden pathway, examining each trinket and toy with all of their golden brass pieces and tarnished metals. In the far corner of the store, a mannequin wearing a long suit jacket with a ruffled white shirt and bow tie solemnly stood in his corner of dust. He was about a head taller than Lydia, and quite skinny. She observed his jacket deeply, noting each pressed seam and flow of the old fabric. The white shirt had faded to a pale yellow and smelled like the pages of an old book.

On the shelf beside him, an old violin case was soiled with water. Lydia unlatched the clasps on the side and creaked it open, revealing a dark, wooden violin.

"Gorgeous," she said to herself, taking it from the velvet and running her hands along the strings. Curiously, she plucked a few, which were loose and out of tune. "How unfortunate."

"Unfortunate?" A voice gasped loudly. Lydia shrieked and dropped the violin back in the case and jumped away. Her head dodged around to find the owner of the voice.

"Who's there?" she called. "I'm sorry, I promise I didn't break anything."

"But you went about touching it!" the voice said. Much to her surprise, Lydia gasped as she watched the mannequin's arm twitch. She dismissed it as merely her eyes playing tricks on her, until the other arm moved as well.

"You just moved!" Lydia pointed to the mannequin, half expecting a reply.

"Well, of course I did! I have limbs, don't I?"

"And you just spoke?"

"I should like to use my voice."

"How on earth can you do that?" Lydia asked fearfully, watching as the mannequin stretched and moved around as if he didn't even know he was an object.

He put his hands on his hips and scoffed at Lydia. "Why are you looking at me so foolishly? You look as if you've seen a ghost!"

"I fear I might have." She stepped closer and placed her hand on his shoulder to prove to herself she wasn't out of her mind. He moved beneath her hand.

He smacked her hand away and scolded, "What are you being so touchy for?"

"Sorry," she muttered. "May I ask how you can speak? And. . .*move*?"

He sputtered, as if to mock her, then replied, "Well, why would I *not* be able to?"

Lydia tilted her head to the side. "Because you're a mannequin. Aren't you?"

"Whatever do you mean? I'm not a mannequin," he insisted.

"Well, I'm very sorry to tell you this, sir, but you quite in fact are."

"Am I really?"

Lydia nodded pitifully and fiddled with her hands. The mannequin sighed and slumped back with a groan.

"I've just awoken from such a deep slumber, I can't seem to remember much of who I am! Is that possible?"

Lydia shrugged, unsure of what to do. What *could* she possibly do?

"Well, why don't you try to remember the simpler detail first?" she said. "Then, perhaps you'll remember the bigger ones."

He thought for a moment. "That sounds like a good idea. Where shall I start? Oh, dear, I can't even think of where to start!"

"That's alright. I can help you," Lydia reassured. "Do you recall your name?"

"Bastien. Sir Bastien Finbar. Oh, joy! Ask me something else!"

"Alright. Let's see. . .did you—or, *do* you happen to have a hobby? A career, perhaps?"

He hummed in thought, then snapped his fingers. "Yes, I remember now! I was—*am*—a great virtuoso. The finest violin player of my day."

"Did you say violin?" Lydia waved him aside with her hand and revealed the old violin she had discovered. He exclaimed with relief and ran his hands along the wood.

"Wolfgang! Wherever did you find him?"

"Just there." Lydia pointed. "Right after I plucked his strings, well, you came to life."

"How odd," he muttered. "And how dare you lay your hands on him!" Bastien waved a nagging finger at Lydia.

Lydia scoffed and retorted, "Well, if I hadn't, *you'd* still be asleep! I didn't know it belonged to you, but even if I did, it isn't necessary for you to be so rude."

"Well, if you'd been dormant for years, wouldn't you be cranky, too?"

Lydia calmed her temper. "Hmm. I suppose I would be."

Bastien hummed with satisfaction, then stretched out his arms and placed the violin on his shoulder, tightening the knobs on the end and plucking the strings back and forth until he was satisfied.

"Much better."

He readied his bow with rosin and smelled it deeply, as if it were familiar to him in a way nothing else was. The bow glided along the strings delicately, shrill at first, then sweet like honey and cream flowing through tea. Bastien swayed back and forth along with the direction of his bow. Lydia swore she heard a sound of movement behind her, but she disregarded it and took a seat on an old stool and admired Bastien's playing. At last, he vibrato-ed a final note, then exhaled a deep breath and stood completely still. Lydia tilted her head and watched as he realized every memory once more. Quietly, he placed Wolfgang back into his case, then plopped into a nearby vintage chair with a defeated look.

"What seems to be the matter, Bastien?" Lydia asked.

He sighed. "I'm afraid I've forgotten most every song I once knew."

"Why, that was the most beautiful playing I've ever heard," Lydia assured truthfully. "You could *still* be the greatest virtuoso of your days."

"You really think so?"

Lydia nodded.

"That's awfully kind of you," he said. "Maybe once more I shall play at the finest balls for the finest of gowns and people."

Lydia suddenly had a wonderful idea.

"I think I just thought of something to help both of us," she said. Bastien leaned forward. "There's a lady in town named Mrs. Fisher, who throws the most elaborate parties around. My family, though we provide the utmost service to her, has never so much as even given us the time of day."

"How rude!"

"I know! She's rather horrid if you ask me," Lydia replied. "Anyways, perhaps if you played for her, she would let *both* of us come to her balls. You could play, and *I* could make a ballgown to prove to Mrs. Fisher she's wrong about my family."

Bastien leapt with joy. "What a wonderful idea! I'll need much more practice before the fact, and perhaps a new suit."

"I'll make you one," Lydia offered. "I'm going to be a seamstress one day, you know."

"You are full of surprises, Miss. . ."

"Lydia. Lydia Mayler." She held her hand out to his and he shook it with such a lovely enthusiasm.

"Pleased to meet you, Lydia. And, I am *very* pleased to be your new partner in business."

Something about this lively mannequin made Lydia feel as if she could do anything. She could be anyone she wanted to be, and suddenly she had the urge to conquer the whole world, sail the seas, and dance in the most intricate ballrooms in the world. In just this tiny, old, somewhat smelly shop, her life had found some sort of purpose. And Bastien would be the perfect one to help Lydia get it.

"I'll need to start on your suit right away," Lydia began, "And then, I'll have to make a dress for myself. . .but however will I afford the fabric?"

Lydia put her hands in her pockets defeatedly, feeling a cold, metallic sensation along her right hand. She gasped and pulled out the golden coin the man on the street had given her.

"Of course! This should be just enough to buy everything we need!"

Bastien clapped his hands, then grabbed Lydia by the shoulders excitedly. "Well, what are you waiting for! Go on, now!"

Lydia nodded, then turned and skipped to the door with her golden coin hanging heavy in her pocket, but as she turned the corner of the store's pathway, she nearly collapsed against a man that she swore wasn't there before. Just before she plowed into him, though, she stopped herself.

"Oh, dear! That would have been the second time this week I ran someone over," she laughed nervously. He was a taller man with dark eyes and brown hair. Incredibly thin, but not frail or too strongly built.

"Oh, hello there. My apologies for the mess. I wasn't expecting visitors." His voice was kind, and he had a very eccentric way about him. He didn't even glance at Lydia. She figured this must be—

"Mr. Miller. Pleased to meet you." He held out his hand behind him as he rummaged through a shelf beside him. Lydia shook it. He continued rambling as he wandered the store, dusting away shelves and tidying misplaced trinkets. He stopped in front of the ballerina, sighed sadly, then returned to his own little world.

"*You're* Mr. Miller?" Lydia said hoarsely.

He chuckled to himself lightly. "What? Have you heard I'm a thief, or some old shyster on a criminal run?"

"No! Well, yes, I suppose, but that's not—"

And, much to Lydia's surprise, he laughed heartily. Her face flushed pink with embarrassment.

"Don't worry," he said. "Just a collector." He picked up a golden book from the shelf and showed it to her, finally looking straight at her. When he did though, something rather strange happened. He gasped and his face became white. The book fell from his hands and landed on the floor with a *thud*. With an array of sputtered words, he tried to compose himself (to no avail).

"Are you alright?" Lydia asked, stepping forward carefully.

"Oh—oh, yes! My apologies, really, sincerest apologies, you just— reminded me of someone."

"Lydia? Who are you talking to?" Bastien came around the corner, but he gasped and froze in his tracks when his eyes found Mr. Miller. For a moment, they only stared in disbelief at each other, until Bastien uttered out a low mumble.

"Hugo?"

He nodded. "Bastien?"

Bastien nodded back. There was one more second of silence, then chaotic friendship ensued. The two cheered and ran and embraced one another excitedly, each frantically speaking over the other with joy.

"It's really you! I was afraid I would never see you again!" Bastien exclaimed.

"I can't believe you're finally awake. It's been *years*, Bastien. How ever did you snap out of it?"

Bastien shrugged dramatically. The man watched Lydia suspiciously. "Did you have anything to do with this?"

Lydia stammered, "I don't know. All I did was come in here and I picked up that violin and plucked a few strings and suddenly he was alive! I meant no harm, I really didn't."

"Harm?" The man echoed. "How could this *possibly* be harmful? My old friend, returned to me at last."

"It must have been her golden coin of luck," Bastien chirped.

The man tilted his head at Lydia. "Where did *you* get a golden coin?"

"A man on the street," she said. "In return for kindness."

He paused, then smiled to himself like he knew something Lydia didn't. He looked at her, then at Bastien, then pulled a golden coin from his pocket. He handed it to Lydia.

"In return for your kindness."

Lydia realized she *had* seen this man before, and it was indeed the very same man she happened to bump into in the street. How unlikely she would (quite literally) bump into him once more.

She smiled graciously and held the coin dearly in her hand.

"Thank you, sir."

"Of course. Kindness is a virtue these days, yes?"

She shook her head yes. "I'm Lydia, sir. Lydia Mayler."

"Oh, yes. A proper introduction." He smiled charmingly. "Vincent Hugo Miller."

"Lovely to meet you, Mr. Miller."

"Please. My friends call me Hugo," he said. Lydia nodded and tilted her head to the side. "Your family owns the flower shop in town, don't they?"

"Yes," she replied. "Have you been?"

"Once or twice." He clasped his hands behind his back. "A quaint little place."

"'Quaint' is just another word for *boring*," Lydia joked.

He chuckled. "Things are only boring when you don't care enough to notice their truth."

Lydia started to say something, but decided not to. She still believed running customers in and out of a shop all day was a pointless way to spend her life, but she knew it would be rude to express that opinion to a shop owner. Bastien excused himself to go practice more, then dipped around the corner. Mr. Miller motioned for Lydia to look around for a while. She agreed, even though she had already wandered along the aisles of the store. But, as she went around this time, she noticed new items and things she hadn't seen before.

She opened up an old jewelry box and pulled out a string of a beautiful flower necklace. A silver chain held rose charms, along with soft yellow daffodils and pink flowers and ivy, wrapping around the chain with delicate color. She instantly knew her mother would absolutely love it.

"Beautiful," Lydia said. "How much is this?"

"That's not for sale," Mr. Miller replied.

"Really? But it's right here." Lydia went to pick it up and show it to him, but when she turned her head it had disappeared.

"Not for sale."

She pursed her lips and nodded, then continued along. Bastien's violin softly emanated through the store. Lydia caught sight of a clock on the shelf, and though it was old, it still ticked, showing the current time of five fifty-six.

"Oh, dear," Lydia sighed. "My mother is going to be so angry with me."

She hurried to the door, frantically waving goodbye to Mr. Miller and thanking him for his kindness and his gift.

"It's a lovely shop," she told him, "You should be very proud."

Bastien frantically caught up with her before she left, and asked, "Lydia! You're coming back, aren't you?"

"Of course I am!" She fixed her hat onto her head. "I promise. I'll be back tomorrow!"

With a final salute, she closed the door and sprinted down Dandelion Lane towards Statesville, then all the way home. Though her feet were tired, she was grateful there was no rain this evening, and she didn't even mind the heavy weight inside of her pockets.

4

Lydia woke early the next morning in order to have plenty of time to purchase fabric for the clothes she planned to make for Bastien and herself. With two gold coins, she could buy any fabric she desired, and the very thought sent a bubble of excitement through her heart. Just imagine! A beautiful gown with golden rose pins in her hair, and the most elegant, poised shoes to go along with it. At last she had something to sew, something to prove to everyone she really could do it. *And*, Lydia had no doubt that her gown would be the most beautiful of them all. So beautiful, in fact, Mrs. Fisher may not even let her into the ball! Lydia daydreamed about strolling up to Mrs. Fisher's large mansion on the seaside and walking straight through those dark, oak doors and into the golden ballroom. All the gentlemen would ask her to dance and she would refuse them all. "I shall escort myself," she would say, "For independence is the most perfected form of elegance for a woman." They would all still try, but she would dance by herself to the beautiful melody of Bastien's violin.

The sun had just risen over the horizon when Lydia set out for the day. The dew settled over the flowers gently, and birds chirped lightly in the air. It was a beautiful, perfect day, and Lydia knew that the coming days would be just as wonderful.

She was one of the first to arrive at the marketplace, just as all the stores were beginning to open. The morning was cool and quiet, and Lydia took a moment to enjoy the crisp scent of air and blossoming flowers. She greeted everyone as she walked by, which wasn't something she would usually do, but she was in too much of a good mood not to share it. The little bell sung when she opened the door to Ms. Maria's Fabric Shop. There were only one or two other people, but that didn't stop Lydia from greeting the shop with open arms and a wide smile. The customers, though slightly confused, embraced the positivity. Lydia scanned the rows of fabric in search of the design that would put all other gowns to shame. Her eyes landed on a golden brocade fabric with shimmery, metallic embellishments. It was thick, but gentle and delicate.

"Perfect."

Along with the base, she found some sheer, soft, golden-creme colored fabric to use underneath it to keep the dress sleek and give it some dimension along with the single pattern. For Bastien's suit, she chose a black cotton and a white fabric that she figured would be very nice ruffled with a long coat and bowtie. Lydia piled all of the fabric in her arms so high she couldn't see over it. The people in the store glanced strangely at her, but she didn't mind. They could whisper all they wanted. Nothing could diminish Lydia's joy.

She plopped the fabric on the counter and peeked around it to see the surprised face of Ms. Maria. Lydia would describe Ms. Maria as a kind lady. Her long, curly black hair cascaded down her shoulders and complemented her brown eyes and dark skin very nicely. Lydia always thought she was a very pretty lady, and thought it very admirable of her to refuse many suitors due to her personal preference of being single. She had been pressured for many years to find a husband, but she always declined, disregarding the judgmental stares and whispers of the rest of the town.

"I'll take all of this, please," Lydia said. She ran her eyes over all of her things to make sure she had everything she needed. "Also, a good amount of matching thread for each of these colors."

Ms. Maria nodded hesitantly and placed the matching threads in a cute little box. She even added in a few sewing needles and tied the box with a bow. Ms. Maria placed all of the fabric in a larger box to fit all of it, then put the smaller box inside of that one.

"Pardon me if this comes off as rude, dear, but how do you intend to pay for all of this?" Ms. Maria looked rather concerned, but Lydia knew she had no ill intentions asking this. Lydia reached into her pocket and pulled out one of the coins. Ms. Maria's eyes grew very wide as Lydia placed it in her hands with a knowing, yet humble smile.

"Lydia Mayler! Where did you get this?" She exclaimed.

"Long story," she said. Lydia gathered up her box. Just before she left, she called back, "Keep the extra!"

Lydia struggled to find a comfortable way to carry the box, but persisted nonetheless. She couldn't wait to show Bastien everything she got, and she already had planned out his entire suit in her head: a black, wonderfully tailored suit coat with silver embroidery and a tastefully ruffled shirt. It surely would beat his current, worn suit and look ravishing along with Wolfgang.

As quickly as she could, she made her way down Dandelion Lane, but to her surprise, the sign was gone. The lettering on the window had disappeared as well, and the curtains blocked any view into the shop. Lydia checked the door, but it was locked. Sitting the box down, she tried to peek through the curtains, but there was nothing to see. Her heart sank. Where could the entire store have gone? How could it have just disappeared? She was just here yesterday evening. They couldn't have completely moved from then to this morning. She tried the door once more, but it was no use.

"Bastien? Bastien are you in there?" She put her hands around the edges of her mouth and shouted. "Mr. Miller?"

The only reply was the chirping of blue birds.

Lydia lowered herself onto the edge of the sidewalk, grateful that the street was empty so no one would witness the deep sadness wash over her. Before she even realized it was happening, she began to cry. For the first time, she felt as if someone made her feel so valued, and they just disappeared. Her dreams were all about to come true, but just as suddenly as they appeared, they vanished. She hated crying, but she couldn't help it. She was altogether just too frustrated.

Why did they leave her here? She couldn't imagine Bastien abandoning her. After all, Lydia was his only hope of becoming a musician again. Could it be that he never even considered her a friend? Or, at the very least, an acquaintance?

"Is it possible that perhaps I made all of this up?" Lydia wondered. Had she really been so lonely that she created a whole new world of characters to love her in the midst of her loneliness?

That couldn't possibly be. Besides, she passed by the store on multiple occasions and it was always there. Cedric and the rest of the town knew about Mr. Miller as well, so it couldn't be that he wasn't real.

Lydia now wished that she had obeyed the promise she made to her parents. She wished she never set foot in that smelly shop full of trinkets, for if she hadn't she wouldn't be feeling so heartbroken.

"So, I suppose you'll just disappear from me again, won't you?" Lydia exclaimed at the empty store. "Well, I really hope you're happy!"

Now, she'd never be able to show her talent and handiwork off at Mrs. Fisher's ball, and she would never have anyone else to talk to besides Cedric, and sometimes Cedric was altogether too serious. Bastien was weird and exciting, and it seemed that at once she knew him, and he knew her. He was unusual and different, just like her, and the whole reason she truly felt so drawn to this treacherous shop was because she understood how the shop felt.

"How silly I must be, comparing myself to a shop." Lydia sniffled and wiped away her tears, placing her head in her hands. She glanced over at the box of fabric and sighed. "Of course my hopes were much too high." The wind blew against her damp cheeks.

Lydia trudged herself back to the flower shop, pitifully carrying the box with her. It was much heavier now than it had been before. She unlocked the doors and tidied everything up, then sulked behind the counter, only being nice enough not to raise any complaints from customers. At one point, Lydia thought she saw Mr. Miller come in, but it turns out it was only a man with a similar looking cloak. If only they had told her they were leaving, she thought.

She wondered where they had disappeared: to great rolling hills filled with flowers and singing birds chasing after clouds? To the grandest of mountains, covered in snow and creatures Lydia didn't even know the names of? Were they in the middle of the ocean somewhere? Sailing alongside dolphins and great sharks? Each curiously upset Lydia further, and she did her best to put it from her mind. They were gone, and it was over. She wouldn't see them again, so why should she sit here and worry?

Besides, it was a stupid dream anyway. To sew beautiful gowns? Arrive at great balls? Be able to explore the world and create great pieces of clothing for the grandest of all kinds of people? How silly. How terribly unrealistic and completely impractical, she thought.

So, she simply watched as the customers came in and out, in and out, and figured she had better get used to it. She would one day end up inheriting this shop anyway, so she might as well learn to love it. *It's a charming shop*, she tried to convince herself, with little flowers, little people, little dreams, so little thought, such little patience, and hardly no drive to give a—

"Excuse me, do you have any roses available?" A customer's voice cut through Lydia's thoughts. She barely looked up at him as she flicked her hand to motion to the far corner.

"Over there."

"Thank you."

"My pleasure." Then she mumbled to herself, "If only."

The day dragged on, just as it did every other day. The clock ticked on endlessly, bringing demanding customers and the occasional rude comment. Lydia wished she could snap and tell them exactly what she thought, but the reputation of her mother was at stake, and if the shop went down so did her family's funds. Today, her mother was busy tending the garden at their house and her father was watching Henry. Once more, the responsibilities fell on Lydia. She didn't mind helping out, but she felt there was so much more of the world to experience than just a marketplace.

Then, just when Lydia finally thought she might be feeling better, Mrs. Fisher strutted in ready to pick up the largest order she had ever placed. Just her luck! Of course Mrs. Fisher just *had* to come in now! Lydia groaned and considered hiding under the counter, but the frilly lady spotted her and waved her down with an expensive fan.

"Lydia, dear! Hello!" She tapped her hands on the counter happily. She smelled of lemon tea and strawberries, and by the large smile on her face, Lydia knew Mrs. Fisher was having a much better day than she currently was. Mrs. Fisher handed her a bag of coins and giggled excitedly. "Your mother said my flowers would be ready today?"

Lydia mustered a smile. "Yes. I'll have them delivered shortly. 415 Dahlia Road, correct?"

Mrs. Fisher nodded and flipped her perfect, curly blonde hair over her shoulder. Lydia made a note to herself and put it next to her on the counter.

"Alright. They'll be at your door by seven o'clock."

"Lovely!" Mrs. Fisher leaned in and grabbed Lydia's head to kiss her forehead dramatically. Lydia held her tongue (and attitude) as Mrs. Fisher pranced out into the sunny afternoon.

Lydia went into the back room of the store to check the order and just as she expected, heaping numbers of bouquets crowded the room. She had absolutely no clue how she would deliver all of these by herself! It was almost five o'clock. Most of the shop owners would be getting ready to close up by now.

"Perhaps Cedric will be bored enough to prefer dragging flowers to the *lovely* Fisher mansion over cleaning dirty shoes," Lydia mumbled under her breath. "How lucky he is."

And so, with a grumpy attitude, she recruited a much too enthusiastic Cedric to help load a flower cart full of Mrs. Fisher's divine bouquets. Lydia grumbled the whole time and "accidentally" dropped a flower or two on the way. She doubted Mrs. Fisher would even notice. Besides, her house was almost a quarter of an hour away. *Some* flowers were bound to fall off eventually.

Cedric helped Lydia tow the wagon down the street and through the open forest trail to Dahlia Road. All the houses each had their own ports overlooking the seaside, sharpening the air with a hint of salt. As if the magnificent splendor of the houses wasn't enough, they just *had* to own nature itself. The two walked down the quiet wood trail, observing the trees and birds chirping about. Lydia shooed away any birds that tried to swoop into the flowers as Cedric helped guide the wagon along the path.

"Really, Cedric. Isn't she horrible?" Lydia kicked at the dirt.

Cedric chuckled and replied, "Aren't you the one who said we shouldn't judge those we don't know?"

"Well, I *do* know her, and I say she's horrible."

"You have the fondest ideas of people in this town," he said sarcastically.

Lydia shrugged and hugged her arms around herself. "That's because they happen to be the furthest thing from fond."

"Why do you despise them all so much, anyway?"

She sighed and shrugged once more. "I don't know. I think I'm just too bored of this town. It's so *dull* and *orderly*. Life isn't supposed to be boring. Is it?"

Cedric nodded, but there was a hesitation in him that led Lydia to believe he was rather sad about the whole situation. He would most likely end up stuck here forever if he didn't stand up for himself, Lydia thought. She couldn't say much, though, because she herself often neglected to speak her truth to her family. After her parents were gone, she was the one expected to continue on with the shop. Henry would never do such a thing, as he was much too immature and would never have any desire to keep up with the garden. So, the hard work and family inheritance fell to Lydia, who wasn't sure what to do about the whole thing. She could keep the shop and just turn it into a sewing shop, but what would her mother think? All of her years of dedication and hard work would be gone in an instant, all because *Lydia* wanted to sew nice clothes.

The trees cleared and opened to a beautiful scene along the ocean. A wooden boardwalk trailed along the edge of the sand and led up to the eccentric homes. Mrs. Fisher's was about halfway down, but it wasn't difficult to distinguish. People strutted in and out in fancy clothes and fine jewelry. Lydia groaned, but held her head as high as she could and beckoned Cedric to the front door.

Knocking passively, Lydia dreaded whatever might happen next. After a moment, Mrs. Fisher flung the door open, wearing a gorgeous red ballgown with glimmering jewelry.

"Oh, Lydia, dear! Thank you!" She tried to kiss her forehead once more, but Lydia dodged it just in time, which then made Mrs. Fisher kiss Cedric instead. He blushed furiously, causing the anger to boil even hotter in Lydia.

"My pleasure," she said through gritted teeth.

***

By the time Lydia returned home, the sun was beginning to set among blue and purple clouds. Her feet ached from delivering the flowers and carrying her fabric all the way back home. She opened the mailbox, sure there would be nothing inside, but a single letter awaited her. Rich, creme colored paper sealed with a wax stamp addressed itself to:

Miss Lydia Mayler

Lydia raised an eyebrow, then sat on the edge of her front lawn and read the note in the little bit of remaining light:

Miss Lydia Mayler,
I hope this letter finds you well. Mr. Miller left it on a street corner in hopes that a passerby might recognize your name and deliver it to you safely.
I am terribly sorry about our sudden disappearance. It is with a heavy heart that I was unable to alert you in person. We shall return in a few days' time, and once we return, I promise to explain all that confuses you. Hugo and I had business to attend to that has been left unsettled for many years now. I hope you understand, and harbor no ill feelings toward either of us.

When the time comes and we must return, I have a feeling that you might be of great help to us. That is, only if you wish to be of service. So, perhaps we'd both be doing ourselves a favor if you happened to wander back into our humble establishment.

Until then, I wish you the finest of days, and look forward to the time I may return.

Sincerely yours,

Sir Bastien Finbar

So they didn't just abandon her! Well, they kind of did, but still! They were out there thinking of her. Lydia sighed with relief, and suddenly her anger melted away. Mostly. She was still partly upset they neglected to tell her beforehand, but it suddenly didn't seem to matter anymore. They *did* care for her, and she still cared about them. They wanted *her* of all people to be at their side. Lydia suddenly felt very childish for having such an ill attitude.

She held the letter to her chest and laughed to herself. How foolish she had been, jumping to all of those conclusions and becoming angry so quickly. Not even the thought of Mrs. Fisher and her ball could upset Lydia now, for she found her hope returned. She prayed they would be back sooner than just a few days, for after they left she was reminded of the boring life she lived. *Anytime now*, she thought, *and then they'll be back.*

"Until then, I suppose I have some work to do."

5

To her disappointment, the shop was still gone the next morning. Mumbling to herself, Lydia brushed off her irritation and made her way back to the shop.

Cedric had the day off, so he stayed around the store with Lydia most of the day. Neither of them did much, but it was better than sitting alone for hours on end, which was how the day was typically spent.

Even still, Lydia spent the free time she *did* have in her room, sewing and pinning and perfecting every detail of the dress she would soon show off to the whole town. She couldn't start Bastien's right away (since she didn't have his measurements and he was so tall and thin), so she continued to work with her own golden fabric. Somehow, she managed to hide all of it from her mother, who was the master of snooping. Lydia sensed Mrs. Mayler's suspicions, but she brushed them off in hopes to lessen the peculiarity.

The next day came and went with no sign of Mr. Miller. Lydia's anger bubbled, but she trusted with all of her heart they would soon return. They *had* to. Because if they didn't, Lydia had no idea what she would possibly do.

So, for the next two days after receiving the letter, Lydia wished the time away in the shop and with every opportunity, she hurried down Dandelion Lane to see if her friends had returned. Every time she checked, though, the empty store mocked her.

Just as Lydia was about to give up, she drug herself down to the shop (expecting the worst), but something changed. When she noticed the swaying green sign and vibrant red letters, her heart leapt from her chest. She ran inside, instantly forgetting every other obligation that bound her to Brightmeadow.

"Bastien! Mr. Miller!" She hurried through the aisles to try to find them, but heard nothing in response. "Bastien?"

A loud crash brought her attention behind her, where Bastien and Mr. Miller stumbled out of a singular old doorway propped up against the wall. After a second of strange eye contact, Bastien leapt to his feet and welcomed her with open arms.

"Lydia! So good to see you again." He brushed the dust off his clothing and helped Mr. Miller from the ground. "I hope you received my letter?"

Lydia nodded. "I did indeed." Then, she suddenly remembered how angry she was. "And you could have told me you were leaving!"

"I know, Lydia, and we're sorry but—"

"Sorry? I had to be sitting around in this *boring* old town while you're out only Heaven knows where!"

Neither objected. "We didn't have a choice, Lydia, we were only trying to keep you safe."

"Well, then it would do you good to know that I would have gone with you," she said matter-of-factly, crossing her arms and turning her head away.

Bastien tilted his head. "You would've? But Lydia, you don't even know where we *went*."

"What does it matter?" She asked, still keeping her pouty demeanor. "I thought you were my friends."

Mr. Miller sighed with regret and pursed his lips. "I suppose you're too upset to accompany us on our next journey, then. Aren't you?"

Lydia perked up a bit, but refused to yield.

"Oh, well. That's such a shame. I guess we'll just have to go to Carmen all by ourselves. What a chore that will be, speaking to the fairies, arguing with witches, you know. The usual."

Lydia eyed him curiously, desperate to interject, but she had to remain strong. She couldn't give in right away, or else they wouldn't take her seriously. She stayed quiet, listening intently to his words.

"Well, Bastien, I fear she's made up her mind. I suppose it's time for us to prepare the doorway to the gardens. Carmen really is such a wonderful place of magic. And that's just *one* of the cities! Never mind that. How lonely it will be, just the two of us."

Lydia could not stand it! She tried to look as disinterested as possible as she uttered, "Magic?"

Mr. Miller smirked and continued, "Oh, yes! And Carmen isn't even the largest of the cities. I dare say it's even our favorite. Right, Bastien?"

Bastien seemed a tad bit confused, but nevertheless played along. "Yes! Carmen!"

"And, hypothetically, what would one have to do in order to go to Carmen?" Lydia asked.

"Oh, I don't know," Mr. Miller said, "Be fearless, curious, have an aptitude for the unknown. Say, Bastien, don't we know someone like that?"

Bastien nodded and glanced toward Lydia as if she wasn't watching. "I recall that we do."

"Alright, fine!" Lydia gave in. "I want to go to Carmen with you!"

"That's the spirit!" Mr. Miller exclaimed. Bastien laughed and twirled Lydia around with glee.

"Oh, you're going to *love* Carmen! It's absolutely beautiful!" Bastien said.

Lydia smiled. "I sure hope it is. But I still don't understand why we have to go in the first place."

The smiled faded from their faces, and suddenly Bastien no longer was filled with joy. His hands fell to his side. Mr. Miller glanced toward his friend, but neither spoke. It was like they were reading each other's minds. Lydia observed them carefully for any indication they could give her of this place, but they said nothing.

"What? What is it?" She asked.

Mr. Miller motioned for her to sit down on one of the chairs behind them. A nervous feeling bubbled in her stomach. Bastien kept his eyes downcast as Mr. Miller spoke.

"This is going to sound terribly strange," Mr. Miller warned, "But Bastien has not always been a mannequin."

"Oh, well I knew that," Lydia said. "He told me he was—*is*—a musician."

Bastien pursed his lips as Mr. Miller glared at him accusingly. "Did he, now?"

"I'm sorry! I know we aren't supposed to tell people, but she was there and I had just woken up, and it all happened so quickly!"

Mr. Miller sighed. "Anyways, what I'm trying to say is—"

"Wait," Bastien stopped him. "Hugo, may I speak to you privately?"

Lydia's eyes glanced back and forth between them.

"Fine. One moment, Lydia." Bastien dragged Mr. Miller away and back behind a corner where they proceeded to murmur back and forth with intensity. Lydia tried to understand what they were saying, but couldn't make out their hushed whispers. She scanned the shelves out of boredom, noticing that many of the objects seemed to have changed locations—all except the ballerina, who still posed elegantly on top of a music box that looked as if it hadn't been played in years. Just as she was about to turn the crank on the box, Mr. Miller walked past her with Bastien.

"That's not for sale," he said, pushing the ballerina further back on the shelf.

"Is *anything* here for sale?" Lydia asked.

Bastien gasped dramatically. "Am *I* for sale?"

"What? Of course not, Bastien," Mr. Miller said. "Lydia, we have something important to tell you, which is something Bastien and I have sworn to secrecy for a long time, now."

Lydia, curious as she was, still had a certain mesmerization with the music box ballerina. Sure, she wanted to know what Mr. Miller had to say, but at the moment it didn't feel very important. She turned the little crank a few times to the side. The two of them hardly noticed she was fiddling with the music box. The ballerina began to spin slowly as its quiet, little bells sung sweetly. Lydia hummed along with it, observing the ceramic dancer twirl mechanically. She was so engrossed in the dancer, she didn't stop to notice the whispers had ceased, and both Mr. Miller and Bastien were watching her in suspense.

It seemed that whenever the music should have stopped, it kept going, even though Lydia had only turned the crank a few times. The ballerina continued spinning and spinning and spinning, until even Lydia was dizzy. Lydia tapped the side of the box and hummed along to the melody. The music ceased at once.

Lydia moved her head back to see the music box and the ballerina, but the ballerina had stopped spinning and had changed her position. Startled, Lydia peered closer, then saw the ballerina move once, twice, then again. Although this frightened Lydia, she was reminded of her first meeting with Bastien, and suddenly she wasn't afraid anymore.

"Can you speak?" Lydia peeked down at the ceramic. The ballerina, though clearly confused, was observing her hands, dress, and hair. She met eyes with Lydia and smiled brightly.

"Oh, dear! I'm awake again! And what good timing, too. My arms were beginning to grow rather tired."

Lydia's eyes grew wide. "I'm Lydia. Lydia Mayler." She held her hands out for the dancer to step into. She complied, and Lydia held her at eye level.

"Lady Antoinette Bellefeuille. Charmed to meet your acquaintance."

Lydia smiled. "Charmed, as well." She turned and showed Antoinette in her hands to Mr. Miller and Bastien. Antoinette gasped at the sight of them. Bastien scooped her up from Lydia's hands and spun her around.

"Antoinette! So good to see you," he exclaimed. "Would you like to go to Carmen with us?"

Antoinette's ceramic cheeks grew bright pink with anger. "Would I! Oh, take me to Carmen this instant! I will have *words* with that witch who turned me into a doll!"

"A witch?" Lydia echoed.

Mr. Miller took Antoinette from Bastien. "Yes, a witch. We were just getting to that. You see, many years ago when Bastien was still flesh and blood, he fell in love with a young lady."

"And I still am very much in love with her," he interjected.

"However, there was a small problem," Mr. Miller said.

"And what was that?"

Mr. Miller pursed his lips. "This witch was interested in Bastien for. . .*other* reasons, but Bastien's heart already belonged to another lady. So, in her jealousy, she cursed him to become a mannequin for as long as he lives." Lydia sensed by the look on his face that Mr. Miller was refraining from all the details, but she dismissed her suspicions.

Bastien cried and sunk pitifully into a chair. Lydia placed a comforting hand on his shoulder as he wallowed in his sadness.

"We aren't sure if it's even possible to return him to his true form, but now that he's awake—thank you again, Lydia—there's a chance we can find the witch and convince her to remove the spell from Bastien."

"How could you possibly convince her? She's a witch after all," Lydia exclaimed, though she retained a small inkling of hope inside of her. This comment only made Bastien more sorrowful, and once again he moaned miserably.

"Witches and wizards aren't inherently bad, Lydia. Only some choose the route of evil," Mr. Miller explained, "Her name is Zabuli, and she herself wasn't always evil."

"Zabuli? That's an odd name," Lydia said.

"Most likely it's a title. It isn't uncommon for witches and wizards to have specific names for their craft. Like a pen name, if you will."

Bastien nudged Lydia and whispered in her ear, "She once tried to curse Hugo, but—!" Mr. Miller shot him a look that discouraged him from finishing his thought.

"She got me, too! Oh, I'll give it to her good if I see her again!" Antoinette steamed. Mr. Miller handed the fiery ballerina to Lydia to handle, because she very nearly jumped from Mr. Miller's hands in a fit of rage. Antoinette huffed and pouted in Lydia's palms.

"The fairies reside in Carmen. They harbor all of the golden dust in our world. Before we even *think* about trying to find Zabuli, it would be in our best interest to have some with us."

"That's it? All we need is golden dust?" Lydia asked. "What makes it so special?" It was only dust, wasn't it? It couldn't be unattainable or, at the very least, priceless. The fairies would *have* to be reasonable and let them use just a few specks of it. After all, it would be used to save the lives of two wonderful people from eternal misfortune.

"You see, magic is a very complicated thing." Mr. Miller skimmed through a bunch of old papers scattered on the store's counter. Beetles and dust scattered from his busy hands. He spoke intelligently, but no hint of condescension crossed his tone. He regarded all of them as equals, and treated them all as such. "There are two different kinds of magic: natural magic and artificial magic. Natural magic is harbored by creatures that are hereditarily magical, such as fairies, nymphs, and the thousand of others. Artificial magic is used by registered witches and wizards. Anyone who wishes to become a witch or a wizard must undergo training at a special school, then attain an apprenticeship with either a specialized witch or wizard." Mr. Miller found the paper he was looking for and took extra care to try and smooth out its wrinkles. "For those who desire to become a witch or wizard, golden dust is required for every spell, because they do not harbor the natural magic to perform spells naturally. Golden dust is the magic that makes the spell work. Does that make sense?"

Lydia, though still confused, nodded her head. From what she gathered, she understood that golden dust was required for spells cast by witches and wizards in order to make the spell work. And, to become a witch or wizard, specialized training was a necessity. She never knew that such people existed in the first place, and it all seemed rather troublesome just to perform a single spell in the first place.

"Is there any difference? Between witches and wizards, I mean."

Mr. Miller nodded. "Witches orient themselves more towards nature and natural things while wizards focus more on the study of spells and the mystic arts."

"I see," Lydia said, but that was a lie. She was very confused.

"Spells and curses can only be broken by those who cast them, which means our best and only hope is Zabuli. Though this frightens me for many reasons, there's not much else we can do."

"Are you yourself a witch or wizard?" Lydia asked.

Mr. Miller finished fiddling with the paper and handed it to Lydia.

This certificate hereby establishes

Vincent Hugo Miller

as a registered wizard with the authority granted

to perform magical spells and enchantments

"A lousy wizard, but good enough to be able to do some simple magic."

"Wow! That's amazing!" Lydia marveled. "Do you cast spells often?"

Mr. Miller chuckled bashfully and shook his head. "I'm afraid not. I don't think magic should replace everyday chores. We have to keep *some* sense of normalcy." He motioned to a dusty crystal ball balancing on a jade platform. "I could see my entire future right here, but what good would it do? You can't change what's meant to be, no matter how hard you try. Magic shouldn't be a placeholder for your life. I like to keep this here as a reminder. You shouldn't be so hung up on changing your future you miss out on the present."

Lydia nodded along, but very well knew that *she* would want to use the crystal ball if given the chance. Changing the subject, she asked, "Do you have any golden dust with you?"

"Unfortunately not. The fairies only allow a certain amount of golden dust to be purchased at a time. Once the limit is reached, they must wait until the next cycle when the spells have been cast or expired. The more magic that's out and in use, the less effect it has. It's important to use it in moderation."

Bastien sniffled again as Antoinette tried to calm him down. Lydia turned away as not to laugh at Bastien's dramatic state.

"Well, let's hope the spell is broken soon to cease Bastien's crying."

Mr. Miller retained his serious demeanor. "Often, it is near impossible to break a curse if left alone for so many years, which both of you here have had that misfortune. To find and convince Zabuli, we'll need as much help as possible."

Bastien sniffled dramatically. "Oh, please say you'll go with us, Lydia. I can't *bear* to go alone!"

Lydia smiled. "Well, you *wouldn't* be alone, Bastien, and you shouldn't fret because I *will* come along with you all."

"Really? You aren't scared?" Antoinette tapped Lydia's hands.

"I suppose I would be lying if I said I wasn't the slightest bit scared, but no matter. I fear being stuck here by myself more than anything. Besides, how frightened will I be if I have you all?"

Bastien blew his nose loudly and sunk lower into his chair with pitiful wails.

"Perhaps frightened still, but it should be just as well. Mr. Miller, I would be happy to help."

He smiled. "That's the spirit! Prepare yourself, for we leave tomorrow!" He scooped an armful of loose papers from the counter and hurried away to unknown business with a skip in his step.

"Tomorrow?" Lydia gasped. "Oh, dear. What will I tell my mother? Or Cedric?"

"No worries, dear," Antoinette assured, "You'll figure it out. Besides, conflict can always be resolved, but it isn't every day a curse can."

"That *is* true. It's settled." Lydia placed Antoinette in Bastien's lap. "I'll be back early tomorrow. Until then, please make sure Bastien doesn't cry himself to death."

"You can do that? Oh, woe is me!" he cried.

Lydia cringed. "Sorry."

6

That night, she could hardly sleep.

Lydia had never felt this way before—so utterly free and excited. She absolutely couldn't wait until the moment she could tell Cedric everything. But what if he didn't believe her? *Oh, nonsense!* she thought. He *would* believe her! Lydia was no liar, and Cedric knew that along with the rest of the town. At *most* her adventures would likely confuse him, but Cedric knew Lydia well enough to acknowledge the fact of her integrity. Lydia was a respectful young lady, and she would never soil her reputation with misleading words.

Still, the idea of Cedric being frightened of her made Lydia feel lonelier than ever. Sure, she had new friends now who were fantastic, but would that really matter if Cedric never spoke to her again? She tossed and turned back and forth all night until the sun peeked over the blue horizon. Though she hadn't slept but an hour and her eyes were heavy and tired, the excitement of adventure overcame any other feeling she might endure.

Oh, dear, she thought. *What shall I tell my mother?*

She supposed she could say she's helping Ms. Maria out, but then Mrs. Mayler would certainly ask Ms. Maria about Lydia later on. Mrs. Mayler would never believe Lydia would help Mrs. Fisher or Ms. Candy on her own, so that was out of the question, too. Who in the world would cover for her?

"Of course," Lydia realized.

Lydia marched herself right down to Mr. Barley's so early the next morning that the doors weren't even open yet. Nevertheless, Lydia knocked on the door (in a bit of a hurry), to which Cedric allowed her in quietly.

"Is everything alright?" He asked.

Lydia smiled mischievously. "Yes, of course. But I must ask a favor from you."

"Anything. What is it?"

"This is going to sound so odd, and I can't tell you why just yet, but if my mother comes around asking where I've been, just say that we were together the whole day. If it's after six o'clock, tell her I went for a walk in the woods near Mrs. Fisher's house to find some wild strawberries and I'll be back before it's dark."

"What? Lydia where are you going?"

The church bell rang six times outside. "I can't tell you just yet, but I will the second I get back. Just promise me. *Please.*"

Cedric thought to himself for a moment, but gave in to her wishes with his kind heart. "Fine. But you owe me."

"I always do. Don't I?" Lydia hugged him quickly, then started out the door to the end of Dandelion Lane.

To her delight, the shop was open. Lydia feared that they might have left her once more, but here they were, waiting just for her. Her heart leapt with joy (and, a tinge of anxiety) as she flung the door open and called out to her friends. Mr. Miller was frantically running around the store while Antoinette sat on the counter looking rather dejected.

"What's going on in here?" Lydia asked her.

"Only God knows! Him and Bastien have been running around all morning throwing things about as if they were getting ready for some *guest* to come in at any moment. Well! What sane person would *ever* bother coming into this place?" Antoinette grumbled. Lydia giggled to herself and put Antoinette on her shoulder, cautioning her to hold on tightly. Mr. Miller stopped his frenzy for just a moment to greet Lydia.

"Good morning to you, Lydia," he said brightly. "I assume you're here for a certain inquiry about Carmen?" He continued to throw things about while he spoke. Lydia very nearly dodged a flying hat being thrown through the air.

"Indeed I am. When are we to leave? I can hardly wait any longer," Lydia exclaimed.

"In just one moment. I can't find my necklace and I've been looking for it all morning." He groaned and ruffled his hair. "I can't leave here without it."

"Why not?"

"The necklace holds all of my keys and charms. We need the keys for Carmen and the store charm to come with us. Wherever the store charm goes, the store goes with it. If it isn't with me, the shop is left unguarded."

Lydia then realized something. "Is that why the store disappeared when you both left? Because the charm was with you?"

"Precisely. I knew I should've just kept it with me instead of hiding it." He then started to speak to himself as if he had forgotten Lydia was there. "Why do I even hide it in the first place? It's not like anyone is going to stop by here and go looking for it." He put his hands on his hips in a huffy, then called, "Bastien!" Bastien stumbled in a flurry with two different ties in either hand. "Have you seen my keys anywhere?"

"Even if I have, that's the least of my concern," he replied, going straight to Lydia. "Which tie do you think looks best?"

"So now we're only worried about our wardrobe?" Mr. Miller grumbled.

"Don't you come for me like that. You're the one who fluffs his hair whenever he walks by a mirror."

Lydia stopped the arguing by averting Bastien's attention back to the ties in his hands. "The dark green one. It suits your eyes best."

He smiled and held it out to her. "Help me out, would you?"

Lydia took the tie and wrapped it around his neck carefully. She practiced on Rosie a lot, even though the dog often protested against it. The rest of the family preferred her in cute dresses, but Lydia found funny ties and brightly colored suits rather amusing.

"There you go." Lydia pulled at the ends gently one last time then gave him a thumbs up.

"Thank you, dearest."

"A-ha!" Mr. Miller exclaimed victoriously, holding a silver chain with keys and charms up in the air. "Found it."

"Finding *anything* in this dump is a miracle," Antoinette muttered with her head in her hands.

Mr. Miller pushed a large, white wooden door out from behind a curtain in the corner. He brushed off some dust from the handle and sighed proudly.

"Perfect."

Antoinette reached her arms out into the air. "Alright. Someone better hold on to me tightly when we go through."

Mr. Miller bit the inside of his lip and leaned down closely to her. "I'm sorry to tell you this Antoinette, but I fear you can't come with us."

"Ridiculous! Why not?"

"You could break, and I'm not taking that chance." He picked up her and sat her on the shelf she came from. "You're too fragile."

"Not as fragile as your ego," she huffed.

"There, there, Antoinette," Bastien comforted, "We'll be back before you know it. Besides, Carmen isn't really *that* great."

"Don't worry, Antoinette," Mr. Miller said. "We'll bring you back a drink from King's Pub."

"Oh, joy! We're going to King's Pub!" Bastien celebrated. When the daggers from Antoinette's eye reached him, he promptly cleared his throat and ceased his joy.

Mr. Miller pulled one of the keys from his necklace. It was long and whimsical and intricate, with metal flowers and ivy wrapping around the handle. There were a few other charms along with the key, like a miniature looking house and a long, slim feather. The silver key's head twisted in the shape of a flower with round petals and a butterfly on the top.

"Is the shop coming with us?" Lydia asked, eyeing the charm shaped like a store.

Mr. Miller smiled. "Of course. Everywhere *this* is—" he held up the charm, "The shop is right there with it."

He stuck the key into the door, which had nothing on the other side of it besides air, and pushed the knob open. Though the door was empty behind it, a strange new world emerged in a breath of fresh, sweet air. Birds chirped in singing voices and tall, green grass swayed in the smooth breeze.

"Lydia Mayler, welcome to Carmen."

Lydia stepped through into the new world of her imagination. Everything was green and alive with all sorts of grass, ivy, flowers, and magnificent trees. Bright red mushrooms sprouted at stumps along stone pathways lining rolling green hills and mountains. In the distance, a waterfall glided over the edge of a rocky cliff. Winged, giggling creatures zipped through the air around Lydia while strange, little creatures waddled at her feet. A few brightly colored animals that looked like large balls of fluff waddled on their tiny paws. Lydia noted that if you looked close enough, cute little faces and tails poked out from either end of their small ears.

Each tree held about half a dozen tree houses, where the winged creatures would fly in and out, leaving trails of shimmering dust that landed in the grass and grew flowers. She assumed these creatures were fairies, the ones of which Mr. Miller spoke. Along with the fairies, there were other sorts of flying creatures: some with human looking bodies, and others with strange, whimsy features.

"It's magnificent," Lydia marveled.

Little gnomes paced in and out of the tree stump doorways with shovels, tools, and funny little hats. Lydia waved hello to one, to which the small, grumpy gnome shooed her away with an obscene gesture. She frowned, but Mr. Miller laughed.

Mr. Miller led them down the stones, greeting each toad, creature, and house he passed by. They all seemed to know who he was, or at least were able to recognize him. A few of the flying creatures followed close by and giggled in hushed voices, but soon gave up on their advances and flew away. Of course, Mr. Miller noticed, yet he only rolled his eyes and smiled. Lydia almost lost him and Bastien on a few occasions because she couldn't stop looking around at the strange new world, but Bastien made sure to keep a tight watch on her.

The more they walked, the more populated the area around them became. Lydia assumed they were headed for a city of some sorts, and could only dream of the creatures and sights she would encounter there. She recalled the name of Seraphina, but that was the most she knew about this place. Lost in thought, Lydia stumbled over a rock on the pathway and almost fell. When she regained her bearings, she noticed a creature standing at her feet: a humble toad, standing on his two legs about two or so feet tall. He wore a cute pink suit and clutched a small, golden harp to his chest.

"My apologies," Lydia spoke to him. "I almost trampled you, poor thing."

He croaked and stared at Lydia as if she was the most magnificent thing he ever laid eyes on.

"Sorry, you can't talk, can you?" She chuckled to herself.

"Actually, I can. But words cannot express the way you look, madam," the toad spoke dearly, bowing to her elegantly. Bastien and Mr. Miller laughed, but Lydia couldn't think of how to respond to that. She wasn't sure what startled her more: the talking toad or the comment he just made. "Allow me to introduce myself. I am Pippin the Bard. At your service, m'lady."

Lydia's eyes grew wide. She laughed nervously and replied, "I'm flattered. Truly."

"Shall I play you a song?" He readied his harp.

"Oh, no, that's alright—" But she was too late, as he already began strumming the silver strings and serenading a flustered (and embarrassed) Lydia.

"Oh and once my eyes did see, the spell a witch once put on me,
To love her til' the end of time, the face of beauty most sublime,
Until she rests her precious head, no sooner will my love be dead,
Golden dust was once the key, for peace throughout eternity,
Now see my sorrows once were bare, wrapped around your golden hair,
Lead me now to glorious days, until my curse will be a haze,
One day I shall soon be free, until then, take my heart, fairest—"

He looked to Lydia as if to ask for her name. He awaited with glistening eyes, holding out for his final strum until Lydia got the hint.

"Oh! Lydia. My name's Lydia."

He frowned and slumped over his harp. "Lydia! The fairest of names, yet it rhymes with nothing!"

She sighed and crouched down to speak to him. "Oh, I'm terribly sorry. I suppose you don't like me anymore, do you?" She said the last bit rather hopefully. Perhaps she wouldn't have to break this poor bard's heart.

"*Like* you? No! I thought I made it quite clear how deep my love runs for you. But woe, I love a woman whose name I can never sing."

She cringed, pitying the poor creature pouting at her feet. Lydia looked to Mr. Miller to help, but he found the whole situation quite hilarious. Bastien was only trying to charm the creatures around him, telling them stories of his days as a musician. He made grand gestures of a violin's bow and Lydia was quite sure he overdramatized most everything about his story.

She motioned to Mr. Miller to come over and whispered, "Can we at *least* bring him with us for a while?"

"What for?"

"Really? Look at the poor thing!"

Pippin the Bard was holding his harp tightly as he rocked back and forth in tears on the ground.

"Honestly, I don't really see the problem here."

Lydia whacked his shoulder with the back of her hand. "Have some sympathy. Haven't you ever loved someone?"

He opened his mouth to say something, then promptly closed it. Biting the inside of his lip, he flicked his eyes back and forth in thought, then sighed and gave in.

"Fine. He can come with us. But *only* for a little bit."

Lydia thanked him, disregarding his strange demeanor. She tapped the toad's shoulder lightly to rouse him from his tears.

"Pippin, would you like to come with us on our journey for a little while? We're going to see Seraphina, you know, and I'm sure she would love to hear a song written for her."

Pippin the Bard sniffled. "Really?"

"Of course."

He loosened up a bit. "Yes. Yes! I will go with you to Queen Seraphina!"

"Wonderful." She led Pippin over to Bastien, who finally had stopped gloating for attention and was waiting for her and Mr. Miller to continue on. "Bastien, this is Pippin. Pippin, Bastien. I should think you musicians would get along well."

Bastien sneered at the harp Pippin clutched to his chest. Pippin sneered right back with judgmental eyes and a jealous *harrumph*. Lydia hardly noticed as she was already beginning to converse with Mr. Miller about where they were going. He told her "straight to the heart of Carmen, where the livelihood of the fairies thrived." He described it so lovingly: magic, fairies, strange little creatures, strange little creatures that could sing. . .

Well, he didn't really need to describe *all* that to Lydia in the first place. She was introduced to that in quite the odd manner. Bastien and Pippin trudged behind them, bumping each other "accidentally" as they walked side by side. Lydia swore she heard rude murmurs between the two of them, but she dismissed it. Pippin would only be with them for a little while longer. Bastien could deal with his problems on his own. Besides, that's what being a real human is all about, and he needed to be reminded of how *normal* humans act. That's what Lydia thought, anyways.

At last, a clearing broke at the edge of the whimsical forest. A path ran through the deep woods and led them alongside glistening waters and tall, dancing flowers. The air smelled sweet like honey and dandelion dust swayed on the breezes passing by. Even in the forest, little wooden houses and shops were strung up in the trees and branches, hanging over the edges of the pathways and inside of old stumps. A small band of gnomes and toads played folk music with harps, strings, and other instruments Lydia was not familiar with. Lydia and the others stopped for a moment to listen. When the others weren't paying attention, Mr. Miller dropped a couple of coins into their funny looking hats. Meanwhile, Bastien continued to do his best to outperform the toad beside him.

"Lydia, you're still sewing a suit for me, right?" He whispered.

Lydia nodded. "Yes. Why do you ask?"

"No reason. I just wanted to be sure you plan on making it a hundred times classier than this *wart's*."

Lydia rolled her eyes and chuckled. "Alright, Bastien."

Lydia thought the band of creatures playing music was one of the most fantastical things she would see, but it turned out that with every step she took, she encountered something even more full of whimsy. Little shops with walls made of sticks and flowers popped up here and there. Saloons were busy with customers inside of large tree stumps with leaf-covered tops and a funky rock for a door. The farther they walked, the louder the sound of running water became. They turned on a pathway with far less population and much more plant life. There were flowers Lydia and never seen before full of fascinating petals, colors, and shapes.

Some were taller than her and others were just the size of her thumb. She reached to pick one off to bring with her, but Mr. Miller shook his head and discouraged her from doing so. Though disappointed, she complied.

Soon they reached a break in the trees. In front of them, a waterfall fell over the edge of a cliff, hiding a pathway across the gap behind it. Lydia gasped at the sparkling water in the lake below, teeming with glittery creatures and strangely colored fish. Mermaids, perhaps, but Lydia could not tell from this high up. Pippin trembled and murmured about a fear of heights. Mr. Miller closed his eyes for a moment, then continued on. Lydia wondered how often he came here to Carmen. She was almost jealous of how accustomed he must have been to it: the fairies, the nature, the perfect rolling lands. How long had he known this place? How long had it been tucked away in that dusty shop? And why didn't Mr. Miller live *here?*

She followed behind him alongside the falling water. If there hadn't been so much gushing over the edge, Lydia would have been able to see straight through. She reached her hand out and ran it through the crispy, icy waters. Even in the shadows, it shimmered and smelled of sweet roses and honey. Pippin trailed closely behind Lydia, whimpering quietly and staying as close as possible to the rocks. Bastien, although just as frightened, put on a brave face to show off. Pippin was so scared the poor thing didn't even mind. Lydia rolled her eyes and continued to keep to herself, quietly observing Mr. Miller and his subtle mannerisms.

The moment their feet hit familiar dirt and grass, both Bastien and Pippin breathed sighs of relief and pretended as if their previous terror didn't exist. Pippin strummed his harp idly, humming words to himself in a sweet, comforting voice.

"I sing to my love of the north wind, a flame that I once did desire,

I grieve of my love from the east wind, whose mourning did put out my fire.

And oh, those past loves of mine, have taken my heart ripped in two,

Now I wonder who'll be, the forever flame in me,

And mend all my broken hearts so blue."

"Your love of the north and east winds?" Lydia asked curiously when he finished. "Who are they?"

"Please think nothing of those, m'lady, for my heart solely belongs to you," he quickly replied.

Lydia giggled. "Oh, I'm not worried, Pippin. Only curious."

"They were both young and fair, chasing after anyone who would court them. I thought my songs would be enough to win their hearts, but in the end they weren't. After they both ran away with different suitors, I never saw them again. I took my own journey and ended up here in Carmen, still searching for the perfect young lady."

Mr. Miller gave her a look that said *I'll tell him if you won't*. Lydia sighed and prepared herself to break this sweet, little bard's heart, but she really just couldn't bring herself to do it. How could she? Even though he wouldn't say it, his heart still hurt over the past, which is something no person can fix.

"It's okay to still be upset over the past, Pippin, so long as it doesn't define who you are," Lydia said.

"I don't know how I could ever *stop* being upset. I suppose all I have left in this world is my harp." He gazed down at his little instrument and smiled sadly.

"You know, Pippin, the only medicine for a broken heart is time."

He glanced up at her wonderfully. "More perfect words have never been spoken."

"Well, Pippin, I am very sorry to tell you this, but I am *far* from perfect," she said.

He shook his head. "Nonsense! Your beauty outshines the greatest of Seraphina."

"No, Pippin." She paused. "Do you know how to tell if someone is *really* beautiful?"

"The way their eyes glisten in the sun and the way their hair falls around their rosy cheeks—"

"No, none of that." Lydia stopped and looked down at his hopeful eyes. "You can tell if someone is truly beautiful by the way they treat people who they aren't the fondest of."

Pippin furrowed his brow. "But both of my loves. . .they were so pretty. . ."

"They may *have* been pretty, Pippin, but that doesn't mean they were beautiful."

The toad clutched his harp to his chest and sniffled lightly. Lydia felt a pang of guilt in response to his sadness, but Mr. Miller gave her a nod of affirmation. Pippin's eyes trailed to Bastien, who was still pouting and ignoring the others out of jealousy. The toad tugged on the end of his jacket. Bastien jumped, then groaned at the sight of the creature staring back up at him.

"Bastien?" He croaked. The mannequin scrunched his nose in the air and pretended as if he wasn't listening. "I'm sure you're a lovely violinist."

Bastien paused, clearly a bit flustered, then regained his composure and jealous demeanor. "*That* is a fact."

Lydia smiled and trailed alongside Mr. Miller, trying to find the words to express her curious wonder. She felt as if she knew who Mr. Miller was for the longest time, with all of the rumors swirling about Brightmeadow and such. Sure, she had heard he could be a thief, a wanderer, a fugitive, or just a strange old man, but she realized that she still didn't really *know* him. He was rather strange indeed, but there was more to his persona and attitude than meets the eye. Or so Lydia thought. Well, much rather *believed*. A man of such attitude and eloquence surely had more to his story than boring old Brightmeadow.

"Why Brightmeadow?" Lydia asked out of silence.

Mr. Miller appeared taken aback. "Pardon?"

"Out of all the wonderful places you know and have seen, why would you choose to stay in Brightmeadow? It *is* the most boring town in the entire world."

He shrugged. "It's safe. And quiet. Both of which are nice qualities when you've had a life such as mine."

"And what kind of a life is that?"

He paused and looked at Lydia, but did not respond. Though curious, Lydia didn't question any further and decided to change the subject.

"So where *did* you and Bastien go? When you left, I mean." Lydia asked.

Mr. Miller replied, "I had to return to Bastien's home to ensure that it was still a safe place to keep on location. Like Carmen, we have a door to get there, but it had been many years since I used it, and I needed to be sure the doorway was intact. I also had a few things I had to return to friends, which I should've done long ago, but that's beside the point. Being forgetful is truly a hassle."

"Did Bastien go along with you?"

He shook his head. "He stayed behind, but because I had the charm with me if he had left the building, he wouldn't have been able to get back in. He can't go back to his home. Not right now, at least. Once he becomes human again he'll be able to return."

"What about Antoinette?"

"What about her?"

"Where is *she* from?"

He smiled, revisiting a nostalgic feeling. "France. One day, I went to see Bastien and his orchestra perform during a ballet performance. Antoinette happened to be the principal dancer. After the show I was waiting by the stage door for Bastien. Antoinette came out before him and noticed a very pushy lady who wouldn't leave me alone. Antoinette stepped in and scared her away from me. She truly has the sharpest tongue and kindest heart of anyone I know."

"She *is* rather fierce," Lydia giggled, "but I appreciate that."

They walked a while longer until a magnificently large tree came into their sight. It was as long as three buildings put together and its trunk reached all the way into the skies. The giant leaves and branches shaded every inch of the mossy, stone ground below. Great roots ripped at the dirt and sprouted along the earth in rugged patterns. A rock staircase led them through an opening in the tree, which revealed a hollowed-out trunk decorated with the finest of things. Lightning bugs lit the halls and ceiling as ivy and flowers hung all around the walls and the top of the corridor. A rug made from moss rolled its way across a tiled floor to a great golden door guarded by two very tall soldiers in ceramic armor. One of them had bright, white hair braided down his back and the other had her brown hair braided away from her dark face. Mr. Miller approached them like old friends, but still retained an attitude of respect and integrity in response to their serious demeanor.

"Good afternoon. I'm here for an inquiry about golden dust with her majesty Seraphina."

"We aren't expecting guests today," the dark headed soldier said. "I'm afraid we must ask you to leave."

"I'm a friend of hers. Just tell her Hugo is visiting."

"Hugo?" The white headed soldier furrowed his brow. "Vincent Hugo Miller, are you?"

"That's right."

The two soldiers exchanged a look in which they revealed they were thinking the same thing. The dark headed soldier raised her eyebrow as if to convince her partner. It must have worked because he then gave a relenting nod. Moving to the side, he opened the door for Mr. Miller and allowed the group to enter into a beautiful courtyard of flowers with intricate statues and fountains. Three fairies shimmered in golden thrones on the top of a delicate, mossy stream of water. Trees hovered above with hanging ivy and golden slivers of light cutting through the air. The flowers seemed to move along with them, glistening with the breeze of the wind.

The fairies glimmered elegantly with long robes and lots of jewelry and gems lining their arms and ears. Lydia assumed the fairy in the middle seat was Seraphina, the one Mr. Miller told her about. She was the most beautiful creature Lydia had ever seen. Long, sleek, black hair twisted around her face and down her sides. Golden, yellow eyes sat against dark, chestnut skin and her arms were embellished with sleek, golden designs. The fairy on her left looked similar, only she had short, platinum hair. She, too, flaunted those golden eyes and striking features. To the right of Seraphina, the fairy had braids streaked with shimmering jewels and gold with a number of rings and bracelets on her arms and hands. Suddenly, Lydia felt very minuscule and humble. Though a bit anxious, she bit her lip and stood with her shoulders back proudly as they approached the throne of Carmen's royalty.

Mr. Miller bowed slightly, but not too far. Just far enough to show his respect and acknowledge her majesty.

Seraphina smiled brightly. "Oh, Hugo. How lovely it is to see you again."

"And you as well, Your Majesty. Carmen is as beautiful as ever."

Pippin stood in awe behind Lydia with a bashful look in his eyes. Though he said nothing, Lydia could tell he was composing a song about their beauty in his mind.

Seraphina looked to Mr. Miller. "You're here for something important, aren't you?"

He nodded.

The queen thought for a moment, then asked, "Dare I ask what you desire?"

Mr. Miller took a deep breath, then spoke with his utmost confidence. "I ask permission to purchase a small sum of golden dust."

"Golden dust?" She raised an eyebrow. "I thought you didn't like casting spells."

"It's for my friend, Sir Bastien Finbar." Mr. Miller moved a nervous Bastien in front of him. "Many years ago, Zabuli turned him into a mannequin, and now he's finally come back to life. We need golden dust to bring to Zabuli to turn him back human. As you know, we fear if we *do* find her, the golden dust she harbors will be laced with black magic. I figured our own, pure dust will do best."

"And what makes you think Zabuli will comply with your request?"

He opened his mouth to say something, then closed it once more. Bastien nudged him, but Mr. Miller only bit his lip and tried to think of something to say.

"I don't know. But she's the only hope we might have of bringing Bastien back to his human form."

Seraphina looked to the fairies on her right and left, then considered her options. Although she was grand and royal, Lydia could tell she considered Mr. Miller's offer very seriously, and took his matter to heart. She could tell the fairies truly wanted to help, but there was something about their reaction that led Lydia to believe they might be out of luck.

Mr. Miller vacillated, "Well?"

Seraphina sighed pitifully. "You know how dear you are to me, Hugo, and how deeply and truly I want to help you and your friend, but we've reached our limit of dust to supply."

Bastien's face fell downcast at her words.

Mr. Miller put a hand on his shoulder and tried to reason. "I understand, your majesty, but I ask that you make an exception only this once."

"You understand the effects golden dust has on magic, Hugo," she said, "If I were to just go on giving out golden dust to *anyone*, magic would have hardly any effect anymore."

"I know, I know. But I come here begging you." Mr. Miller pursed his lips, then smiled to himself. "And, I say this as respectfully as possible, but I do believe you owe me a large favor. Don't you?"

The queen's breath caught in her throat as she turned to the fairy with platinum hair. She nodded in response to Mr. Miller's words with an agreeing smile. Seraphina ran her hand along her chin, then sighed in defeat.

"You leave me no choice, Hugo." She clapped her hands to motion for a guard. "Iano, please bring Hugo here a vial of dust. *Only* one vial."

"Thank you, from the deepest depth of my heart." He reached into his pocket and sifted through a variety of coins in a bag. "How much?"

Seraphina waved her hand. "No charge. Just this once. In return for kindness."

Mr. Miller glanced to the platinum haired fairy, who smiled warmly at him, almost as if she were saying *thank you*. He acknowledged the fairies one last time with a bow, then said his goodbyes and led the group out of the garden and back into the forest. The sun still hung at its peak in the sky. Despite the weather being perfectly wonderful and the sun beating down at the earth below, it was neither blistering hot, nor humid and dry, but exactly the temperature it ought to be.

The four of them traveled back the way they came. Pippin and Bastien continued their passive aggressive arguing all the way back, even after Mr. Miller had glared at them quite obviously a number of times.

Lydia found their whole dynamic amusing. Mr. Miller, who was an eccentric, charming man and Bastien, a dramatic musician with no filter. They were the most unlikely of friends, but Lydia could tell they cared for each other more than any other friends she had seen in her days. In a way, they reminded Lydia of her and Cedric. Cedric being the dramatic, happy-go-lucky one with a kind personality and Lydia being more apt for things most people didn't understand. Maybe that's why Mr. Miller seemed to trust her so much. They really weren't all that different when she thought about it.

At long last they reached the doorway that led back to the shop on Dandelion Lane.

"Well, Pippin, it was nice knowing you. So long." Bastien flicked his jacket and started back into the doorway, but Pippin protested.

"Wait a minute! You can't just leave me here."

"You live here," Bastien deadpanned.

"Well, that's true, but. . .but I could help you!"

Bastien opened his mouth to disagree, but Mr. Miller held up a hand to stop him.

"How so?"

Pippin croaked. "Well, among the three of you, I'm the only purely magical creature, which means I have a special gift."

"That is true. . ." Mr. Miller raised an eyebrow. Lydia furrowed her brow in confusion, to which Bastien then explained to her, "Every creature who is hereditarily magic has their own special magical gift. You know, like the power of healing, or the power of speaking in tongues."

"So. What's your gift, then?" Mr. Miller asked.

Pippin hesitated. "I don't know."

"Ha!" Bastien laughed. "You don't know!"

"*Yet*! I don't know *yet!*" Pippin slugged his shoulders. "I haven't figured it out."

"What a shame. Goodbye frog. Hugo, Lydia." Bastien turned his nose up in the air, expecting the others to follow him back into the store, but they didn't. Lydia and Mr. Miller glanced at each other, clearly thinking the same thing. He reached his hand out to the toad.

"Any sort of magic can help us," he said. Bastien groaned, but Mr. Miller cut him off. "And, we *are* on the hunt for the benefit of *Bastien*, aren't we?" The mannequin grumbled in response, yet understood Mr. Miller was right. "Good. Now that's all settled, back to the shop we go. Come along now, Pippin."

So, the three of them stepped back into the shop of curiosities with a new and unlikely friend. Well, friend to *two* of them. Bastien was still refusing to speak to the poor toad, which was probably a good thing. If there was anything they didn't need right now, it was another problem.

Mr. Miller locked the door to Carmen and lit a lamp on the counter to bring some light into the dim shop. Outside, the sky began to grow dim with pink and purple hues. Lydia sighed, knowing if she didn't return home soon her mother would have her head. She desperately wanted to tell Cedric everything that had happened, but she would have to wait until the morning.

"Tomorrow then?" She observed her friends with a smile.

Mr. Miller nodded. "Until tomorrow do us part."

And as Lydia skipped down the empty roads under the setting sun, she had never felt such a joy on the streets of Brightmeadow.

7

"Cedric! Cedric!"

Lydia held onto her hat tightly, the wind whipping at her dress and hair, as she raced towards Mr. Barley's shop.

She had jumped out of bed much earlier than usual due to the fact she couldn't sleep from her excitement. It didn't matter to her, though, because her wildest dreams were nothing compared to Carmen.

Lydia pushed through the people on the street and burst into Mr. Barley's shop. A flustered Cedric drowned in a sea of screaming, angry customers. Lydia pushed past them all and grabbed Cedric's hand. He tried to hand out the orders to the snapping fingers and waving hands, but it seemed the more he did, the more chaos ensued.

"Lydia, I'm afraid I'm much too busy right now for an adventure. Perhaps a rain check?"

Lydia grumbled, but retained that perfect excitement behind her eyes. "No, you're never too busy for this."

She grabbed his hand tightly and pulled him around and into the back of the store, only causing the complaining crowd to become more irritated. Cedric held a hand up to say, *one moment!* then followed Lydia into a back room that smelled strongly of leather and polish.

"Lydia! What is the matter?" Cedric tried to look annoyed, but his kind demeanor gave away his facade. Lydia could hardly speak her words as she was so excited and still in a great wonder of all that had just occurred.

"Do you remember when you told me to stay away from Mr. Miller's shop?"

"Yes?"

"Well, I didn't do that, but—" Cedric opened his mouth to scold her, but she promptly cut him off with a hand. "Don't look at me like that! If only you could have seen the things *I* have seen!"

"A couple of rusty tools and used tableware?" He said sarcastically.

Lydia smacked his arm. "*No*, Cedric. It was like—there were—and —" Lydia acted out big motions with her hands, but couldn't seem to string together the thoughts and visions she was trying to convey.

"What a lovely picture." Cedric rolled his eyes.

"It's just—ugh!" Lydia put her head in her hands, then suddenly got an idea. "What if you came with me? Today."

Cedric scoffed and laughed in an almost mocking manner. "Lydia, come on."

"What?"

"I'm not—Lydia, I'm not going to that strange place with you. In fact, I'm rather inclined to believe you yourself never went there."

Lydia raised her eyebrow and stepped back. "You're saying I lied?"

He sighed and ran his hand along his chin. "Lydia, you can't expect me to believe—"

"No," Lydia interjected, "It's fine." It wasn't fine, and she was hurt, but she was too upset to speak to him any longer. "I'll just go by myself, then. Or not, because *apparently* I'm a liar now. Hmm. Maybe I'll also go *steal* something on the way home."

She stormed back into the impatient crowd of customers as Cedric tried to call her back in. The bell on the door jingled fiercely as the slammed it behind her. It was a good thing the sky was cloudy and cool, because Lydia was absolutely steaming. If she went home, Cedric would follow her there and she would have to explain everything to her mother. If she stayed in the marketplace, Cedric would certainly find her there, too.

Only one option prevailed, so Lydia made her way to the end of Dandelion Lane and quietly entered the store no one else dared to.

Suddenly, everything was quiet.

She leaned against the door and took a deep breath, letting the quiet sound of wood creaking under her feet be the only thing she heard. She felt like crying, but she fought away the urge and harbored a deep anger instead of sadness. Lydia never lied, and even if she *did*, the last person that would be to is Cedric. How could he be so quick to assume?

Lydia sulked behind the counter in a dusty chair and watched the clock's hands tick by. She heard footsteps approach her, but she didn't bother to turn around.

"Tough day?" Mr. Miller asked.

Lydia nodded sadly and put her head down on the counter.

He sighed and pulled a chair beside her. "May I ask what happened?"

Lydia shrugged. "A friend of mine thinks I'm a liar. *Me*. A liar! I'm sure pigs can probably *fly*, too."

"Well, *some* pigs can."

"Really?"

He nodded. "But that's beside the point. Why does he think you're a liar?"

"Because the truth is always so improbable." Lydia stuck her bottom lip out and pouted.

"Truer words have never been spoken."

"You know, you really aren't making me feel any better," Lydia said.

Mr. Miller shrugged. "Is there something that you wish that I would say?"

She mimicked his lazy shrug. "I guess I just wish there wasn't so much expected of me."

Pippin, who had been asleep on a small, faded chaise, woke at Lydia's words and stretched his little, webbed feet. "Oh, don't worry, Lydia. You're a perfectly wonderful person."

"He's right, you know."

Lydia smiled weakly. Though she was still upset by Cedric's words, she figured thinking about them would only make it worse. But she just couldn't get them out of her head. . .

"I know what'll cheer you up," Mr. Miller said. "How about I tell you what we're doing next?"

She perked up a bit. "That sounds interesting."

From seemingly nowhere, Bastien came stumbling into the scene, disheveled and pouty.

"Has *anyone* seen my silver bowtie? I can't find it anywhere." He dumped out a bucket full of metal trinkets and coins, then rummaged through the drawers behind the counter. "Hugo, I swear if you don't make this place *half* decent. . ."

Mr. Miller didn't seem too bothered by his comment. He dismissed Bastien with a wave of his hand and a sly grin. Bastien grumbled and continued throwing papers and strange objects in the air. "Nothing! I can't find anything in this place." He threw his hands in the air with defeat. With one last sigh, he pulled out a slip of paper sticking up from the drawer bursting with scraps. He unfolded it and read it just to do so, but when he saw the words his eyes widened ever so slightly.

"'To Vincent Miller, in the case you ever change your mind and desire to see me once more—sincerely Zabuli.' *Zabuli*. Why do you still have this?"

Mr. Miller took the note from him and read it quickly, then dismissed it as if it weren't important. "I don't know. This is from many years ago, but I'm sure I must have kept it for a reason. . .a memoir, perhaps? No, that's too obvious." Bastien rolled his eyes. All of a sudden, Mr. Miller gasped and perked up. "It's a reminder! Take this, Bastien." Mr. Miller shoved the note back in Bastien's hands and started searching messily through the hoard of papers, fabrics, and trinkets bursting out of the shelves. He mumbled incoherently to himself, tossing things mindlessly behind his back (which Lydia and Pippin had to dodge). Unfortunately, Pippin didn't move hastily enough when an oversized thimble came flying out of Mr. Miller's hands, and it bonked him right over the head.

Little puffs of smoke popped out here and there, sending bundles of papers and coins splattering all over the floor. Mr. Miller went through dozens of pieces of worn parchment, throwing them over his shoulder when they didn't catch his interest. "Where on *earth* did I put it?" He muttered.

"Is he *always* this disorganized?" Pippin murmured to Bastien and Lydia.

Bastien shrugged with a worried expression. "I hope not. Imagine what he must have done to me when *I* was stiff."

At last, Mr. Miller held a roll of parchment victoriously in the air.

"What's that?" Lydia looked at the ink scribbled on the paper.

"An incantation. Well, expired incantation, but a clue nonetheless."

"Expired?"

He ran his finger along the words and spoke in a hurry. "Spells that you purchase from witch vendors—mostly the spells on the simpler side—have a date that you must complete them by. Otherwise, the magic will fade away. The quicker you use them, the more powerful they are. This one in particular I had to let expire on purpose." He held the paper up for the rest of them. "You see, it's a revelation of Zabuli's location. If I had let the magic fade away in here, she would still be able to feel a draw to this place. I couldn't keep her essence here, it's much too dangerous. If the spell expired here, she would be able to find us in an instant. Same with this—" He held up the store's charm from his necklace. "If she ever got her hands on this, we'd be goners. But now that it's finally time to use this spell, I'll need to use golden dust to reactive it. Lucky for us, Seraphina has already granted us that permission."

"Where did you let the spell fade away, then?" Bastien questioned.

Mr. Miller smiled. "Bart's swamp. See the mud on the edges?"

"You tricky basta—" Bastien chuckled, but Mr. Miller cut him off.

"Careful there, Bastien."

"Bart's Swamp! Say, I have some friends there," Pippin said.

"Don't you see?" Mr. Miller exclaimed, "*This* is how we can find Zabuli! I'll use the golden dust we just got to renew the spell. Once the magic is restored, we'll be able to complete it and figure out where she is."

"Oh, joy!" Bastien exclaimed.

Lydia then realized something. "But. . .you're saying you *bought* a spell? From *Zabuli*?"

He shrugged. "I needed to be able to find her somehow. After I heard what she did to Bastien, I tricked her into giving me this spell to find her. Honestly, I'm quite shocked my plan worked. I suppose finding her will be much more difficult now, though. She certainly has it out for me."

He flattened the paper out on the desk and read it out loud:

"Flowers bloom through drying light, but never do they see the night,

Along the coast of what is known, below the surface of your own,

Past Rolling Hills and skies so blue, I gift this spell of clues to you,

One more place will remain unknown, until you find my dearest home."

"What does that mean?" Lydia reread it over. "Flowers? Coasts? Skies?"

Mr. Miller folded it back up and stuck it in his pocket. "Isn't it obvious? We must travel to places of which she described and find a specific magical object from each location."

"That was obvious?" Bastien furrowed his brow.

"Hush, Bastien, I'm thinking." Mr. Miller closed his eyes and rubbed his temples. "So, once we find the magical object from each of these places and put them together, we'll know where Zabuli is. Ha! And they say I'm a lousy wizard."

"You're the *only* one who says that," Bastien replied, but Mr. Miller ignored him.

"All we have to do is figure out where these somewheres are. It might just work in our favor that something in this very shop could help us."

"Somewhere?" Lydia echoed to herself. "How can *somewhere* be in a place that's already here?"

"Ugh," Pippin groaned. "You're making my brain hurt."

Mr. Miller knocked on Carmen's door. "Similar to this door, which just happens to be incredibly convenient, some of these objects are more than they appear." He smiled to himself. "Bastien! Give me a minute. Lydia, make yourself comfortable." And, in a hurry, he ran around to the end of the shop to rummage in all the junk. Although he was on the opposite side, Lydia and Bastien could hear the clanging and throwing of things. Clouds of dust and cobwebs scuffled through the air and over the shelves.

"Well, I suppose now is as good a time as any." Lydia opened the top drawer of the counter and dug around for a slip of paper and some ink. Lucky enough, she spotted a measuring tape in the corner of the desk.

"How exciting!" Bastien leaned in closer and whispered only so Lydia could hear: "It *will* be better than Pippin's, won't it?"

Lydia sighed. "Like I said, whatever you want."

"Oh, joy!"

So, while Mr. Miller caused a ruckus around the store, Lydia ignored the loud disturbances and scribbled Bastien's measurements onto a wrinkled piece of parchment. Pippin gazed at her unabashedly as she did so, but she tried her best to pretend she didn't notice.

"Bastien, when's the last time you played for a ball?" Lydia asked.

Bastien perked up confidently, then shut down just as quickly. He frowned and laid his head in his hand. "Come to think of it, it's been quite a while. I suppose I'll need some practice before I get back out there."

"If it makes you feel any better, I've never even been to one. I'll have to learn to dance all by myself."

Bastien waved his hand. "Oh, don't worry about all that dear, it's rather simple. You just follow your partner here and there and hang on tightly when they dip you."

"I wish I could say that sounds dreadful, but that would be a great, big lie," Lydia joked. "I once heard Mrs. Fisher *hires* people to come dance at her parties to make her acquaintances feel shameful and poor in her presence."

"She sounds delightful compared to others I know."

Lydia chuckled and wrapped the measuring tape up, then placed the paper in her pocket. "All done. I must say, it might be a while until it's ready."

"No worries. It's not like I have much to do in the meantime."

"Actually, I'd say otherwise." Mr. Miller appeared once again holding a dusty frame outlining a painting of a garden. Pink roses and white chrysanthemums decorated the canvas with a small cottage in the distance. If any place were to hold magic, Lydia thought, surely it would be this piece of art. "The gardens of Goya, a quiet little place a dear friend of mine once painted for me. Well, there are more ways to get to Goya, but this here is a nice little shortcut."

Pippin swooned at the sight of the painting as Bastien examined the edges coated in dust. "What does this painting have anything to do with Zabuli?" Bastien then gasped as if he realized something. "Unless?"

Mr. Miller nodded and cleared a place on the wall to hang it up. "'Flowers bloom through drying light, but never do they see the night.' The Gardens of Goya. Paintings hold eternal sunshine and youth. I just can't remember what I did here."

Bastien tapped his shoulder and whispered something into his ear. Mr. Miller frowned and grew quite exhausted looking at once. Bastien tapped his fingers anxiously as the man contemplated his reaction, leaving Pippin and Lydia confused.

"Never mind that," he finally said. Clearing his throat, he continued, "There is a special breed of flowers associated with magic in these gardens. Pecuflos—a pink flower with golden trim and a wonderful conductor of magic—*exclusively* found in Goya." He pointed to the pink flowers in the painting. "The trouble is, because of its magical properties, it's extremely difficult to find among all the pink flowers here. We'll have to go deep into the painting to find them."

"*Into* the painting?" Lydia echoed.

"Problem?" Mr. Miller raised an eyebrow.

Lydia shook her head. "No. I don't think so, anyway."

"Great. Bastien, would you like to go first?"

"We're going *now*?" Lydia fiddled with her hands nervously. Though she had just been to Carmen, a place beyond belief that defied everything she once knew, an anxious flutter bounced around in her heart. She had no time to even prepare herself for this new adventure, and she still wasn't really over her argument with Cedric.

"When else would we go?" Bastien tilted his head.

"I don't know, it's just. . ." What was it? Why was she all of a sudden holding back? It was clear that Cedric would believe what he wanted to believe. No matter what she told him, his mind was made up. It was partly freeing to her. She could truly do what she wanted and not worry about Cedric hovering over her shoulder every second. He always seemed to be there when she made risky decisions. Not to control her, but it was almost as if he felt the need to keep a watch on her. It bothered Lydia that he felt it was his responsibility to take such an initiative. Lydia was a clever girl, and she didn't need Cedric to *babysit* her. Besides, this was exactly what she dreamed of. Mystical lands, far away places, daring adventures. . .

"Can you show me how to step inside of it?"

Mr. Miller smiled. "Like so."

He pressed his hand gently against the frame, tracing his fingers along each flower. He tapped once, twice, then three times in a row, and suddenly he disappeared. Lydia peered into the painting and saw the outline of a painted Mr. Miller waving to them.

"Me next!" Pippin did the same as Mr. Miller, and soon he was sucked right into the paint as well. Bastien followed suit.

"Well, I suppose it's my turn," Lydia chuckled, but she really was nervous. She shook away the feeling and took a deep breath. What could go wrong?

Slowly, she placed her hand in the center of the painting and tapped her finger once. Then twice.

"Here goes nothing."

Three times.

A cooling sensation rippled over her skin, like water engulfed her whole body at once. She closed her eyes and braced herself until the feeling faded away. When she opened her eyes, the scenery around her looked as if a brush had painted everything. The tree leaves were dabs of paint, the streams of water had colors cascading down the rocks, and her friends were all painted images of once normal looking people. Well, somewhat normal. Bastien *was* a mannequin, and Pippin—well, Pippin wasn't even a person in the first place.

When Lydia looked down at her hands and dress, brush strokes replaced once smooth skin with an array of colors and patterns.

"Magnificent," she murmured to herself.

"Alright, everyone, focus: we're looking for a Pecuflos flower. Every other flower here will have silver lining in the petals. Pecuflos has gold. That's *very* important."

"How many do we need?" Pippin asked.

"Just one will do," he replied. "And remember: do *not* pick *any* other flower from the painting. If the painting is altered in any way, it will be destroyed, and we'll be stuck here forever."

Lydia's heart fluttered.

"Bastien and I will look over there, by the stream." Mr. Miller pointed behind him to where a stream ran through some trees and bushes. "Lydia, Pippin, are you both okay to look around here by the cottage?"

Pippin nodded enthusiastically.

"Alright, then. Good luck to you all."

Bastien and Mr. Miller headed off to the stream, leaving Pippin and Lydia among the bushes. She didn't mind. She enjoyed Pippin's company. Besides, she figured it was good for Bastien and Mr. Miller to have time to themselves to talk. Years of being separated probably took a large toll on both of them.

"Isn't this magnificent?" Lydia said with awe, admiring her dress which had become intricate brush strokes. "We're quite literally a masterpiece."

"I didn't think there was any way for you to become more beautiful," Pippin sighed.

Lydia laughed. "You flatter me so. Come along, now, we have a flower to find."

So, Lydia and Pippin dug through the thick bushes in search of the Pecuflos, which seemed to be nowhere in sight. It was also very difficult to pinpoint any difference among the flowers because each was slightly muffled by paint, and the only difference they had to their advantage was a small sliver of gold. So far, Lydia had only found silver in the flowers. Pippin had pointed a few out to her to double check, but none of them passed.

"This is much more difficult than I thought it would be." Lydia wiped a hand across her forehead. "Any luck down there, Pippin?" Pippin had moved a few yards over to cover more ground, but it didn't help. He shook his head *no*. Lydia sighed. "Well, crumpets."

Pippin wandered back over with a hopeful sort of look. "Don't worry. We'll find it sooner or later."

"I suppose. I just hope it turns out to be sooner."

"Don't we all." Every time Pippin spoke, there was a certain kindness in his voice that Lydia loved to hear. Truly genuine.

As Lydia lost herself in thought, she hardly heard Pippin wonder aloud, "What about this one here?" as he reached his hand to pick a flower. The words finally registered.

"Pippin, no!"

But it was too late. The flower separated from its stem with a snap, and its silver lining faded to dust. Pippin gulped.

In the distance, a white cloud flurried over like a storm of dust. It devoured the colors in its way and covered the sky with dry smoke. Mr. Miller and Bastien watched fearfully as it grew larger. They ran to Lydia and Pippin, Mr. Miller clearly annoyed.

Lydia glanced to a vision to her left and just happened to notice a flower glowing with golden lining. Just before Mr. Miller herded the group together and sprinted to the door, she managed to pluck it from the bush.

The cloud bellowed towards where they were standing. Pippin shrieked and dropped his flower. Lydia grabbed his hand and caught them up to Mr. Miller and Bastien.

"Faster! Come on, now!" Mr. Miller called.

The white storm grew closer and closer and even closer until it was barely scraping their heels. Lydia reached her arm out to catch the door handle. Just a few more steps. . .

The knob connected with her hand and the second it did she pushed hard, sending the four sprawling onto the dusty floors of the shop. The door slammed behind them as they crumpled onto the ground in a giant, tangled ball.

For a moment, they all lay there in silence, glancing at each other with shocked expressions not knowing what to do next. Then, Lydia began to laugh. She didn't know why, but it just happened. The more she thought about how ridiculous this whole situation was, the harder she laughed. There they were: a singing toad, a mannequin, a lousy wizard, and the daughter of a florist all crumpled in a heap because they picked a flower in a painting. The whole thing struck Lydia as terribly funny, and all at once she felt so alive. Soon, the others joined in on her laughter until she clutched her stomach and could hardly breath.

"I can't believe we just did that," she exclaimed. "All for a flower."

This only made the others laugh harder. Bastien sat up on his hands to catch his breath. "I know I'm still a mannequin, but I haven't felt that alive in ages."

"What a return to the good old days," Mr. Miller chuckled. Climbing to his feet, he tilted his head and admired the painting once more. He didn't appear angry or upset in the slightest, which confused Lydia. "I've been looking for an excuse to get rid of this memory. I suppose life has done the chore for me. How convenient."

He took the painting off the wall and admired the dusty white canvas one last time before tossing it behind his desk with the promise of ridding it forever. Pippin breathed a sigh of relief with the knowledge that no one was angry with him, but he still appeared upset.

"I didn't even get to keep the flower," he sighed.

Lydia chuckled and patted his head. "That's alright, Pippin. I'm sure we'll find plenty more that are just as beautiful." An idea crossed her mind. "Say, my mum is actually a florist. Did you know that?"

He shook his head no, but a gleam of interest crossed his smile.

"Why don't I bring you a bouquet and you can choose your favorite?"

Pippin nodded his head excitedly, already forgetting his disappointment.

"Perfect."

By now, Lydia had also forgotten about her past upset. Cedric was nowhere to be found in her thoughts. All she could think about was the escape from Goya, a true adventure that her heart yearned for. Did she enjoy almost dying? No, of course not, but the thrill that came along with it was exhilarating. Would she do it again? Definitely not, but she certainly would spend the rest of her life chasing the same feeling as she did when she crumpled onto the floor of Mr. Miller's shop and laughed until her stomach hurt with her best friends in the world.

Bastien helped Lydia to her feet as she flicked the dust from her dress. A few stray strokes of paint were still on her arms and legs, but they would wash off easily. Lydia half-hoped they wouldn't. She thought they were beautiful, and they served as such a wonderful reminder.

The sky outside dimmed to a pale pink color with white clouds floating against the line of shops and trees in the distance. Lydia couldn't see it from here, but she knew the ocean always looked rather beautiful at this time.

Mr. Miller observed the spell from Zabuli again as he flattened out some more crinkles. Lydia remembered the flower in her pocket and quickly took it out and handed it to him. He smiled with an impressed tilt of the head.

"Good work."

Lydia shrugged as if it were no big deal, but deep down she felt very proud and loved the validation the others gave her. "No big deal, really."

He pulled a mason jar from one of the desk drawers and blew the dust and spiders out of it. Once it was empty, he placed the Pecuflos flower inside of it and sealed it tightly.

"One down, two to go," Mr. Miller said. "The more objects we get, the stronger the spell should come. Now, 'along the coast of what is known, below the surface of your own.' Pray tell, what could that possibly be?" He spoke as if he already knew the answer, which Lydia and Bastien assumed he did. "What is something we are familiar with, yet resides alongside our own knowledge?"

"A loving gaze?" Pippin said.

"No," Mr. Miller replied, hardly noticing what he said. Bastien snickered, to which Lydia then nudged him with her elbow to hush. "'The coast of what is known' is the *ocean*. And, lucky for us, I know just the way to get there."

"Don't we live right by the water?" Lydia raised an eyebrow sarcastically.

"We do." Mr. Miller examined the flower with an intrigued eye. "But I mean the *real* ocean."

As usual, a fearful gulp came from Pippin, contrasting the excited outburst from Bastien.

"It's been so long since I've gone," Bastien marveled. "Tell me, Lydia, has it changed at all?"

"I don't think so," she replied.

"Tomorrow it is." Mr. Miller picked Pippin up and threw him in the air with excitement. "May the morning serve us well."

* * *

That night, Lydia sewed carefully in her bedroom, squinting through the dim light of the moon and a lantern on her bedside. Her hands ached and her fingers had been pricked one too many times, but she couldn't bring herself to stop.

"Lydia?" Mrs. Mayler knocked gently on the creaked open door and entered. Lydia quickly threw all of the fabric underneath her bed before her mother could see. "What are you doing in here?"

She shrugged. "Nothing."

Mrs. Mayler eyed her suspiciously, but didn't push her any further. She came and sat on the edge of Lydia's bed. Lydia bit her lip nervously and looked down. "You know there are no secrets you have to keep from me."

Oh, dear, Lydia thought, *there are plenty of secrets to keep from you.*

"I know."

Her mother sighed. "It's just—you've felt so far away lately. I just wanted to make sure everything is alright."

Lydia nodded enthusiastically. "Yes. All is well and wonderful."

"Good. I worry about you, you know."

Suddenly, Lydia felt very guilty about the whole thing, and realized that if her mother ever found out all she was hiding, she would absolutely lose her mind. In Lydia's mind, it was no big deal. It was just an everyday thing. A routine. It had become her new normal, and *wow* did she enjoy every moment of it. Mrs. Mayler, on the other hand, *certainly* wouldn't feel the same. She was as protective as any mother would be, and held Lydia to a higher standard than most people her age. Lydia didn't mind, as she often found herself rising to the occasion, but for once in her life she wanted to chase after something with her heart. *Not* with her head.

"You haven't a thing to worry about." Lydia smiled innocently.

Mrs. Mayler tucked her daughter's hair behind her ear and kissed her forehead. "Good night, Lydia."

"Good night."

The second she left the room, Lydia snatched the fabric from the ground in a hurry to see that a small rip interrupted the bottom seam—a rip that would soon have to be mended before it grew too large to repair.

8

The first thing Lydia figured she ought to do the next morning was to speak to Cedric, but she couldn't deny the bitterness still harbored within her. She pretended as if she *wasn't* bothered, but that wasn't the truth. Eventually, she'd *have* to speak to him again, sooner or later.

She hoped it was later.

Before she left, Mrs. Mayler had breakfast waiting for the family in the kitchen. When Mrs. Mayler made breakfast, it was usually followed by a favor (often aimed towards Lydia). Lydia tried to sneak away before her mother saw her, but it was no use. She dragged her back to the kitchen table and sat her down with an annoyingly cheery smile.

"Go on, eat your breakfast," she said, "It'll give you energy."

"What would I need all this energy for?"

"Well, I was *hoping* that you could watch the store for me today. Henry tore his last pair of trousers and I need to go fetch him some new ones."

"Can't father take care of the flowers?" Lydia asked with a mouthful of tea and biscuits.

"No, he's watching Henry. And don't talk with your mouth full."

Lydia gulped. "Sorry." She sipped some tea. "I can't go to the store today."

"Why not?"

"Because I'm—" She caught herself. What could she say she was doing? It had to be something believable and *somewhat* significant. If it didn't matter, then Mrs. Mayler would make her work. If it was too far-fetched, then she would never believe her. "I'm. . .going to the sand coves with Cedric."

The sand coves were a nice little spot on the beach-y side of town where a lot of people liked to go buy sweet treats and drinks and sit on the sand to watch the waves.

"Really? That sounds lovely."

"Yes, and I do believe he's already there waiting for me. I'm running late as usual," Lydia added on. The perfect thing to say! If there was one thing Mrs. Mayler despised, it was being late.

"Oh! Well, don't let me keep you. I'll just open a little later today."

Lydia knew exactly how to play her next card. "Are you sure? I'm sure Cedric will understand if I have to cancel. It really isn't that big of a deal. There's always tomorrow. But I think he has to work until the end of the week. . .it doesn't matter. I can just tell him I'm busy."

"No, no! It's no worry, dear. Besides, I have to go restock more yellow carnations. We'll be just fine. But *tomorrow* you have no choice. Consider yourself obligated."

Lydia smiled innocently. She groaned internally at the thought of having to work the next day, but was grateful for her current victory. "Thank you, mum. You're the best." She reached up and kissed her cheek lovingly. "Good luck finding Henry trousers. I'll be home later in the evening."

"Be careful, dear, and have fun!"

Well, the time to talk to Cedric came sooner than Lydia expected. She would, of course, have to ask him to cover for her. Lydia knew he would, but a part of her felt the slightest bit guilty. She wasn't *using* him, she was only just. . .asking a favor. That's what friends do. Right? *She* would do the same for Cedric if he ever asked, so why did she feel so guilty about it in the first place? Lydia thought about it, then concluded it was caused by the lack of time they had together recently. Usually, they were around each other all the time, but lately things had been different.

Before she left her front yard, Lydia remembered Pippin, and she made sure to pick an array of flowers for the especially curious bard.

The town was just beginning to open up and come alive when Lydia arrived at the doors to Mr. Barley's shop. She knocked politely, then waved to get his attention when she saw him sulking around inside. With an obvious groan, he opened the door and grumbled, "We aren't open yet."

He tried to close the door on Lydia, but she caught it just in time. "I know, sir, but I just need to speak to Cedric for a moment."

"He isn't here."

"What?" Cedric not at work? That was a rare occurrence. "Where is he?"

Mr. Barley sighed. "He's spending the day with that Arden girl. Something about being family friends."

"Caroline Arden?" Lydia echoed. Cedric, not going to work and spending the day with Caroline Arden? *She* was *a nice girl*, Lydia thought. Though Lydia was aware their families were well acquainted, she found it rather off Cedric had declined any mention of Caroline before. "Did he say why?"

"Why would I ask? I don't care," he grumbled. "Off with you now."

"But, sir, wait, I—" Before she could get a word in, Mr. Barley shut the door in her face. Lydia groaned and mumbled a few unkind things under her breath. Cedric spending the day with Caroline? Something about that felt a little . . . *off.* Why wouldn't Cedric tell her what he was up to? Well, now that she thought about it, she *did* remember earlier that her and Cedric hadn't had their usual time together, and Lydia also had new friends of her own. She only prayed that her mother didn't go snooping around and question Cedric when she discovered Lydia was not by his side.

Actually, this could all work to Lydia's advantage. Caroline *did* look very similar to Lydia, which would sometimes cause confusion in the older folks in town. They both had the same curly hair and kind smile, something Cedric often complimented Lydia on. If Mrs. Mayler happened to see Cedric, she would see Caroline as well, which she would most likely assume would be Lydia!

So, under the cover of a doppelgänger, Lydia turned down Dandelion Lane to her next adventure. When a familiar figure approached her in the street, though, she should've known better than to assume the day would go by perfectly.

"Good morning, Lydia! You're out and about early." Mrs. Fisher struggled to wave Lydia down from a distance as she carried about a dozen bags in her thin arms. Lydia felt a headache coming on.

"Good morning to you, Mrs. Fisher."

"I haven't seen you working in the shop lately. What have you been up to?"

"Oh, nothing," she replied. "Nothing at all."

Mrs. Fisher smiled sweetly, the kind of smile that always made Lydia's stomach turn. Something about it seemed so fake and icky, almost like she had something to hide behind it.

"Well, I best be off. I have company on the way. Cheers, for now." Mrs. Fisher dismissed Lydia at once and continued her walk as if she hadn't even seen her in the first place. Rolling her eyes, Lydia made sure no one was watching as she entered the shop on the end of the street.

Mr. Miller was drinking a cup of tea beside Bastien at the counter while Pippin and Antoinette focused intensely on a game of cards. It was a very different atmosphere than the usual chaos.

Lydia, still annoyed by the troublesome Mrs. Fisher, plopped in a chair across from Mr. Miller and huffed, "I'm honestly quite inclined to believe that *some* witches are just born naturally!"

"Not possible, but please elaborate," Mr. Miller said.

"That horrid Mrs. Fisher!" Lydia exclaimed. "All she does is boast about her *wealth* and *rich* company. Honestly! Her whole personality resides in that giant house of hers!"

"It *is* a known fact that some witches like to live in large castles." Mr. Miller shrugged.

"I wish she would just leave us all alone. Ugh! She really just knows how to ruin someone's day." Lydia crossed her arms and continued to pout, but felt a flower stem poke her in the side. Her mood improved in an instant as she moved to sit cross-legged next to Pippin and Antoinette.

"Good morning to you both," she said, "Who's winning?"

"I just did." Antoinette sat down a final card with a triumphant smile, to which Pippin groaned and threw his cards on the floor.

"Third time in a row!"

Antoinette laughed to herself. Lydia took the flowers out of her pocket and handed them to Pippin. "I thought you might enjoy these."

Pippin's eyes widened as he smelled the sweet arrangement. "These are beautiful! Your mum really has a gift with nature. Are you sure *she* isn't a witch?"

Lydia laughed and shook her head. "No, Pippin. She just loves to garden. And she's very good at it."

"I can tell." He observed each flower carefully, noting each color, texture, smell and petal. "I don't know if I can choose a favorite."

"That's alright. You keep them and let me know when you figure it out."

Lydia stood and moved back to where Mr. Miller and Bastien were lounging. Bastien was busy tuning Wolfgang while Mr. Miller sipped his tea calmly and watched.

"I don't suppose we'll be leaving soon?" Lydia asked hopefully.

"Ah, yes. Soon we shall." Mr. Miller hardly moved and poured himself another glass of tea.

"Care to say where we're going?"

"The ocean."

"I know," Lydia said. "But there must be more."

"Perhaps."

Lydia groaned and leaned her head back. "Why must you torment me?"

He thought for a moment, then smiled. "Fine." He sipped the rest of his tea down. "Somewhere."

"That's helpful."

"No, *Somewhere,*" he repeated.

Lydia groaned. "Saying it over and over again really isn't helping."

"We're going to a place *called* Somewhere."

She opened her mouth to say something, then closed it once more. "Got it."

She got the idea that not even Mr. Miller was entirely sure of what to expect, so she ceased her questioning. Though excited, she convinced herself it would be more fun to know less of what to expect so there would be more of a surprise. Her heart started to beat a little faster with anticipation.

With a final sip of his tea, Mr. Miller *aahed* with a satisfied smile, then turned and double checked his hair and vest in the mirror. He talked to himself frantically as he circled around the store for no apparent reason.

"The ocean is rather grand indeed. . .is it just the ocean? No, it couldn't possibly be, it must be land. Just as I read—but—no, I couldn't—*wouldn't*—have read wrong. I'm not *that* stupid . . . "

"How are we going to get there?" Lydia really only asked him this to draw him from his thoughts, but it worked. His head fluttered a bit, then he clapped his hands and motioned for them to look closely at something he pulled from his desk drawer. He placed a metal dragonfly with shiny wings on the table. "On this."

Lydia blinked. "Say I'm crazy, but I don't think we can all fit on that."

He chuckled, then clutched it in his hand. "Come with me. Bastien, Pippin, you come along as well. Once again, my sincerest apologies. We'll be back before you know it, Antoinette."

Antoinette pouted, but didn't argue. Lydia helped her back onto the shelf before the three of them followed Mr. Miller through the back of the store and outside to a small, grassy area. A tall fence blocked the view of other shops and hid the yard from sight. The grass had grown all the way up to Lydia's knees and weeds devoured the edge of the fences. Mrs. Mayler *certainly* would not have approved of the shabby state of the yard.

Mr. Miller put the dragonfly on the ground, then bent down and fiddled with the side of the wing. At once, it expanded to a much larger size. Now, the dragonfly was large enough to see each intricate detail. On its back, there was a seat towards the front with levers and a steering wheel, and in the back there were two seats very close to each other. Its wings flapped lazily.

"Think we can all fit, Lydia?"

Lydia rolled her eyes playfully. "I suppose we can." She poked around and examined the flying dragonfly. She glanced up at the sky with a curious look. "Won't everyone be able to see us on this strange thing?"

"Not at all," Mr. Miller replied. "To those below us, we appear as a small, simple dragonfly."

"How odd," Lydia murmured, running her hand along its long wings.

"Well, there's no more time to waste. Buckle in, everyone. Oh, and one of you will have to hold onto Pippin," Mr. Miller said.

"I won't have a seat belt?" He croaked.

"No. There's only two seats. See? Oh, don't look so worried you'll be fine."

Though fearful, Pippin climbed onto the dragonfly in-between Bastien and Lydia's feet. He tried to hang onto Bastien, but he was promptly shunned. Lydia let him hang onto her boot and promised if the ride became too bumpy, she would hold on to him tightly.

Mr. Miller ruffled his hair back, then climbed into the front seat and started to switch and push levers and buttons.

"Aren't *you* going to use a seatbelt?" Lydia asked.

He shook his head. "Don't need it. I'm used to this."

He yanked the lever to his right down hard, which then caused the wings on either side of them to rapidly flap up and down. They moved so quickly it created a blur of color in the air.

"Everyone ready?"

Lydia nodded excitedly. Bastien did the same. Pippin, on the other hand, only whimpered.

"Alright." He pressed his foot down against the pedal below the steering wheel. "Here we go!"

The dragonfly lurched straight into the air, sending the three behind Mr. Miller back into their seats with a strong gust of wind. Lydia laughed as they flew up into the sky, higher and higher. Pippin held on for dear life. The wind blew back her hair and it felt as she were a bird, flying to great places she had yet to travel to. She reached her arms out and hollered. Mr. Miller glanced back and smiled as Bastien did the same.

"This is incredible!" She exclaimed, looking down at the shops and people of Brightmeadow. "Look! There's my mum's shop, Pippin!" Lydia pointed down at the small building, but Pippin had both of his eyes squeezed shut out of fear. She giggled and continued to marvel at the grand height they achieved. Soon, they passed over the sandy coves. Lydia's smile faded from her face as the reminder of Cedric flickered in her mind. She shook it off and closed her eyes as Mr. Miller accelerated the dragonfly higher into the sky until they were flying amidst the clouds. She reached her hand out and ran it along the white curtains. They were cold and wet, which wasn't what Lydia expected. It was like sea foam, but also a million, tiny, static needles pinching at her skin.

Mr. Miller pushed a button on the steering wheel that set the dragonfly steady. He swirled around and smiled wildly at the three behind him.

"See, Pippin? It isn't that bad."

Pippin was whimpering and hanging onto Lydia's leg with all of his might.

"I'm sure he's fine," Mr. Miller reassured.

"This is amazing!" Lydia grabbed a handful of cloud. "How often do you fly like this?"

"Anytime I want," he said.

"I've always wanted to know what it was like to fly." Lydia closed her eyes and sighed. "I'll never have to wonder again."

And suddenly, the same feeling she got when she was crumpled on the floor crying with laughter returned. Her heart swelled and she could've sworn any moment she would cry because she was just so full of joy. She was so weightless. It was a feeling that most people would only enjoy once in their lifetime. How lucky she was to chase after a feeling and find it just as she supposed she would.

The plane dipped lowly underneath the clouds, revealing the grand ocean with no hint of land in sight. Lydia marveled at the sight of infinite water and glimmering waves. She lived right beside the ocean, but she had never seen it like this before—in its most raw and elegant form: completely and utterly blue and open, waves dancing below, and creatures lurking underneath the crashing water. Below them a little bit of a distance Lydia spotted a yellow boat of some sort with strange windows and staircases along the sides of the walls.

"What a strange looking ship!" Lydia marveled.

The wind carried them for a little while longer. The air was fickle, changing from cold to warm to freezing whenever the dragonfly would move in a different direction. The wind smelled of salt and sometimes, if she looked closely enough, Lydia could see the fins of dolphins peeking out from the surface of the water. Bastien seemed to be enjoying the ride as well. Lydia figured if Pippin wasn't hanging on for dear life, he might've enjoyed it, too.

"There's *Somewhere*. Right over there." Mr. Miller pointed to an island with white sands surrounded by opaque water with purple crystals on the bottom. He landed the dragonfly on the edge of the beach. The four stepped off and regained a dizzy balance in the thin sand. Pippin shook and whimpered, and was all too grateful to be back on land. Bastien snickered at his fearful eyes. "I've only ever read about this place. Flew over it a few years ago, though. Never got around to exploring it. Come along now. I believe I know what we're searching for."

"What would that be?" Lydia asked.

"Verunda." He brought through the sandy trails into a forest of rocks and ivy with purple flowers blooming about. "The purest water in the earth. So pure, it forces the drinker to tell the truth of their heart, even if they resist."

"Do. . .do we have to drink it?" Lydia vacillated. Though she knew pretty well what her true thoughts were, she often felt as if she skimmed over the negative ones. The ones that made her realize her wrongs. She shook away this fear. She had nothing to hide in the first place. Well, besides the fact that she was lying to her parents. That wasn't really a secret she tried to hide from herself, though.

Mr. Miller halted, as if he hadn't thought of that. "I'm not sure."

Bastien shrugged. "I'm an open book. I don't think there's much I think of that I don't speak out loud."

"How lucky you are," Lydia teased. Pippin didn't seem too concerned with the whole matter, which Lydia figured wasn't a huge deal to him. Like Bastien, Pippin said most everything that crossed his mind.

Mr. Miller said nothing else on the matter. All at once he grew very stern and refused to joke with the others as he usually did. Lydia dismissed it as nerves, but she wasn't sure what he could possibly be nervous about. He knew more about this place than the rest of them did. *Surely* he wasn't frightened.

They came upon a great cave made of crystals and stone. The inside was lit with lightning bugs guiding the path with golden gleams. The group followed Mr. Miller down the cavern. A shiver went down Lydia's spine in response to the sudden cold. Her breath appeared in front of her and the hairs on her arms stood on end. Pippin clung to his vest tighter and shivered.

An opening at the end of the cavern invited them forth, covered with swaying ivy and thick leaves. Mr. Miller pushed the leaves aside and entered into a domed room with a pool of water in the middle. The dome was only a few feet above their heads, covered with shining lightning bugs and glimmering stone and quartz. The pool was rather small, but the water was so clear and pure you could see to the very bottom. It shimmered with a sweet hum of silence. The air smelled sweet, like sugar and cold air on a foggy morning. Her reflection stared back at her in the water.

A quiet hum drew their eyes to the opposite side of the pool. A very tall woman with white hair and pale eyes ran her hands through the water. Her skin was like milk, and her eyes looked as if a thousand memories were trapped inside of them.

"I hear visitors." Her voice was deep and smooth—rich like dark chocolate. "It's been a long time since I've had those. Be a dear and tap the water for me, would you?"

Mr. Miller tapped the top of the water with his finger, sending waves over to the woman. She tilted her head, then moved her hand and face towards the rhythm of the ripples.

"There. Gentle hands, gentle spirit. I can feel it." She smiled kindly, her head bobbing along with each dissolving wave.

"Who are you?" Mr. Miller spoke with a certain wonder in his voice.

The woman raised a hand to her heart and tipped her head subtly. "I am Gara, the blind seeker of truth." She tapped her hands against the water. "You're here for my water."

"Yes," he replied, "We need it for a spell. You see, my friend Bastien here—"

She raised a finger and opened her mouth as if to say *ahh*, with a knowing smile. Her finger tapped the air. "I sense a broken heart."

"Well, as I was saying, Bastien fell in love, but then—"

"No, not from the cursed one." Gara closed her eyes and took a very deep breath. "From the one who touched the water."

Mr. Miller grew very pale at once, then removed his hand from the pool and quickly dried it off on his shirt. Lydia eyed him curiously. Bastien said nothing.

"If you desire truth from others, you must first be honest with yourself," the woman said. Her hair flowed elegantly behind her bare feet. The rings and bracelets on her hands jingled whenever she waved her hands through the air. Her every move flowed as if she were in water: slowly, yet so sure of what she would do next.

Mr. Miller swallowed hard. "I don't understand."

A smile creeped along Gara's face. It wasn't cynical or judgmental, but true. Genuine. Gara didn't strike Lydia as evil or ill-intentioned in any way. Her voice was kind and her aura calm. She was only a bit strange.

"Drink."

Mr. Miller's eyes wavered towards the rippling water that seemed to be alive with magic. All at once, the Mr. Miller Lydia knew was gone. He seemed so young all of a sudden. Yes, he was already young, but it was now the kind of young you see in someone Lydia's age. An innocence being broken for the first time. The kind of young where you know you're supposed to be better than you are, but you just don't want to be, because you're good enough for yourself and that should surely be enough. The lively, charming Mr. Miller was now stared petrified at the pool of water in fear.

"Go on," she whispered, "You have nothing to fear." She leaned in closer, and even though she was across the way from them, it felt as if she whispered right into his ears. "*Gentle spirit.*"

He shook his head. "I don't want to." He glanced up at her with helpless eyes. Gara paused and considered this.

"Then you shall leave as you came—with nothing." She turned her back and waved her hand to dismiss them, but Mr. Miller abruptly changed his mind. Sighing defeatedly, he bit the inside of his lip in thought. "Fine. I'll drink it. But *only* me." Gara raised an eyebrow. "Don't make the others suffer."

Though hesitant, she agreed with a subtle nod.

With shaking hands, Mr. Miller lowered himself to his knees and leaned forward into the water. The eyes of his reflection watched him accusingly. His hands cupped together. Hesitantly, he leaned forward and drank a long sip from his palms.

For a moment, nothing happened. Then, all at once, something within him changed. He fell back from the water and took in a deep breath with dry lungs. His eyes turned red. His knees caught him as he fell back and hunched over himself. Hair hung over his face and hid him from everything he so desperately tried to hide. Bastien rushed to help him, but Gara stopped him with a hand.

"I know you mean well, but let him be," she spoke. Though she was blind, she knew everything destined to happen moments before the rest of them did.

Mr. Miller's breathing slowed at last. His hands held his head with delicate strength. Gara pursed her lips as if she already knew what was bound to happen. Lydia figured she *had* known, which caused a deep anger to ignite within her.

"Can't you see he's hurting? Make it stop," Lydia called to her.

"Oh, darling can't you tell?" Mr. Miller shivered in the cold beside her. Gara laid a gentle hand on his back to calm his shallow breathing. "His pain hasn't *ever* stopped."

The strange woman dipped a quartz vial into the water. She popped a cork in it and felt her way over the other side of the pool using the pathway of crystals and rocks on the rocky walls. Crouching beside Mr. Miller, she laid a single hand on his head, and suddenly his breathing smoothened. Gara moved his chin up with a gentle hand. He watched her with tired eyes as she held the vial out to him. He accepted it, never breaking sight with her white face.

"You can be free whenever you choose to be," she said. "But only if you choose."

The walk back to the dragonfly was the quietest walk of Lydia's life. Not even Bastien uttered a single word. Mr. Miller avoided looking at any of them directly, hardly even breathing.

No one spoke of what happened on the way back home.

* * *

The familiar quiet of the shop gave Lydia a calming sense of peace. After all that had happened since the morning, she felt as though peace was the furthest thing from her mind. From Cedric, to Mr. Barley, to whatever just happened in *Somewhere*, Lydia had the sudden fear that maybe she *had* dreamed all of this up in her mind. A tug on her dress reminded her otherwise.

Lydia crouched down to a concerned looking Pippin. "Do you think he's alright?"

The second they had all entered back into the shop, Mr. Miller disappeared from sight. Bastien seemed to know where he went, but he didn't follow. He only said that it was best if Mr. Miller stayed alone for a while. Though Lydia felt guilty about not inquiring about his well-being personally, she understood Bastien probably knew best.

"I'm sure he's alright, Pippin. We all have bad days."

He nodded, then said his goodnights and curled up on a giant, oversized pin-cushion (free of needles) near the corner of one set of shelves.

Lydia bit the inside of her lip and made sure Pippin was asleep before whispering to Bastien, "Is he alright?"

Bastien sighed and hung his head. "I'm sure he's fine. I know what he saw, and it's probably best if you didn't inquire any further about it."

"What did he see?"

"As I said, it's better if you don't ask."

She nodded, but still thought to herself of a way she could possibly figure out what was going on. As she turned to leave, Bastien pulled her back once more.

"I know now is certainly not the best time, but. . . do you have it finished?"

Thankful to have something else on her mind, she replied, "I'll bring it tomorrow afternoon. I'm being forced against my will to work until closing. There's one more thing I have to fix, and then it should be ready."

He smiled. "Lydia Mayler, you are an angel sent from above."

Pippin awoke at these words and glared jealously. Lydia rolled her eyes playfully and crouched beside him.

"You know you'll always be my number one," she teased. Pippin crossed his arms and pouted, but it certainly made him feel better, even if he didn't show it.

* * *

By the time Lydia finished Bastien's suit, the moon hung at its peak in the sky. Her eyelids weighed heavy on her cheeks. Whenever she sewed, time seemed to slip away from her. Often she would forget she was even sewing and her hands would end up moving on their own as her mind focused on the craftsmanship at her fingertips. It truly was a gift to love something that most people would consider a chore.

Her dress was close to being finished as well, but she had to finish the outer layer with shimmering lace and the stitches on top. She had extra fabric she used to make a pretty hairpiece with as well. Deep down she wished she could show her family what she was working on, but she knew that would lead to further questioning, which would only expose all of her secrets.

Lydia also realized that eventually her secrets *would* be revealed, whether she was the one to do so or not. The clock ticked mercilessly. She prayed her family would never find out about her lies. Lydia was *not* a liar, but she knew deep down that everything, no matter how good, must come to an end. Even the best of times can not last forever. The past events of the day certainly proved that.

Secrets revealed. . .it wasn't *just* her that hid her sorrows on the inside. Lydia had never really thought about Mr. Miller being scarred by something. Not that she didn't think he had *emotions*, but he always seemed so . . . content. Now and again she had questions, but for the most part he was a charming, happy person. A dear friend. Desperately, she desired to know what Mr. Miller hardly knew about himself. Of course she understood how inappropriate it might be to ask, but why was he so secretive about it in the first place? Were the rumors about him around town *really* true, or was it something more?

No matter. She didn't need to think about all that now. Besides, it was time for her to rest. She dreaded work in the morning. The more time she spent away from her mother's shop the harder it was to go back. She got a taste of the life she always dreamed of, and now she was back to the life that bored her so. She had no problem helping her family out. That was her responsibility and her pleasure. But the thought of remaining on Magnolia Street for years to come absolutely terrified her.

9

As Lydia had expected (rather dreadfully), the store was busy with people the second the doors opened. She partially regretted staying up so late last night, but she knew it was worth it. Her work paid off. Now, she had a different kind of work to worry about.

Customers rolled in and out. Within the first hour of being open, all of the pink roses and blue carnations sold. She wasn't surprised. Those were usually the first to go.

Lydia kept a tiny needle nearby so whenever she began to fall asleep, it could prick herself back awake. Her mother left tea in the back for early mornings, but it did little to help keep her awake. It also didn't help that she had no time for breakfast that morning.

The bells outside rang eleven times. Lydia shook her head awake. Eleven already? She must have fallen asleep at some point. Time felt like a deep sludge of water, rolling back and forth lazily on the tides. She rubbed her droopy eyes and stretched. The sun shone bright and hot through the windows, which didn't help her fatigue in the least. She always enjoyed the peppy customers, who called her *dear*, or *honey*, and the older ladies that called her *sugar*. When sleepiness overcame her though, so did grouchiness. Lydia had to remind herself to be polite multiple times, as she was not only representing her own reputation, but her family's.

A man in a cloak sauntered up to the counter. Lydia couldn't see his face. At first she hardly even noticed he was there. The needle pricked her and jarred her awake. He *psst* quietly. She glanced around at the store with only about a dozen customers, then at the strange man on the other side of the counter.

"Um. . .may I help you, sir?" She asked. Two eyes peeked from the hood along with a familiar smile. "Bastien! What are you doing here?" Lydia leaned across the counter with a worried expression.

"Coming to rescue you from work!"

"Oh, dear," she groaned.

"No worries. We'll get you out in no time." He nodded his head towards the door. Lydia chuckled and rolled her eyes, then leaned back against the chair. Bastien whispered to her again, but she dismissed him with a wave of the hand.

"Bastien, I *can't* go right now. I have to work."

He frowned. "You're no fun."

"No, I'm not. In fact, I have a very special gift where I take all the fun out of a room," she gibed. When people eyed her strangely, she cleared her throat and resumed her usual position. "I'll be there later today."

"Fine," he pouted, "I suppose I'll have to speak to *Pippin*." He started to walk out, then turned his head back to see if Lydia would stop him.

She shrugged. "I suppose you will."

He groaned, then flung the door open and left. Lydia giggled to herself, then started to put together a bouquet from some old flowers behind the desk. Sometimes she would give them away at the end of the day, free of charge. Only to the nice customers, though. Often to children. There was a little boy who liked to come in with his mother. What was his name again? John? Matthew? She couldn't recall, but he enjoyed making petite flower crowns and placing them on stray cats outside when they came up to him. Every so often a stray cat would wander inside and fall asleep in the display window with flowers hanging round its neck. It really worked nicely.

Just as Lydia began to give in to her desire for sleep, the smell of leather and mahogany wood tickled her nose. She lifted her head from her arms on the counter and saw Cedric's grand smile. He held a brown bag in his hands, which smelled of tomatoes and strawberries.

"I do believe I owe you a lunch."

She smiled weakly. "Thank you."

He pulled a chair from around the counter and sat opposite of her with happy eyes. Lydia tried to act as if her fatigue wasn't so terrible, but there was no hiding the fact she only got a teaspoon of sleep.

"*So*," Lydia drew out. "*Caroline* Arden." She raised her eyebrows playfully at a now very red Cedric.

"What about her?"

"A whole *day*? I heard you even bought her a croissant. With *strawberries*."

Cedric crossed his arms defensively. "It's *polite*. Besides, we're only friends."

She giggled. "Sure. That's exactly what Philip Davidson said about Laura Andrews. How many kids do they have again?"

Cedric scowled and bit into his sandwich hard.

"Can we talk about something else?"

Lydia rolled her eyes. "Fine. Keep your secrets."

"Speaking of secrets," he said, "What about you and that mystery on Dandelion?"

"What about it?"

"Have you. . .gone back?" He said the second part as if it were some scandalous feat.

Lydia smiled to herself. If only Cedric knew the half of it! She feared if she told him the truth though, he would only become angry, and the news could possibly spread back to her household. "No, I've just been. . .you know. . .out?"

He furrowed his brow, somewhat unconvinced, but said nothing to contradict her.

"I feel as if I haven't spoken to you in weeks."

Lydia breathed a sigh of relief. "I'm so glad I'm not the only one who felt like that."

Cedric smiled shyly. He looked down bashfully and shook away the blush rising in his cheeks. Lydia was confused as to why he was so shy all of a sudden. All she said was that she missed his company. They were *friends*. Why was that such a strange thing?

"Lydia, may I ask you—"

Before he could finish what he was saying, a flustered man ran into the store with watery eyes and a frantic voice, speaking quickly and nervously about how he needed a dozen roses at once. Lydia chuckled internally, knowing it must be a turmoil with a lady, and fixed him a set of roses with a discount. He thanked her graciously, then hurried right back out. Lydia laughed, then recalled Cedric sitting rather nervously by the counter.

"Sorry about that. What were you saying?"

He made a face as if he had forgotten. "Oh, nothing."

She furrowed her brow and smiled slyly. "Alright, then."

Cedric watched her carefully, leaning a little closer as if he might say something important, then stopped. He shook his head, gathered up his things, then said goodbye a little too quickly. Lydia barely had time to wave as he ran out the door.

* * *

Though tired, Lydia managed to drudge down Dandelion Lane with the nicely wrapped box containing Bastien's suit. Half of her wished to go home and sleep, but the other half of her was just too excited to wait another moment to see how perfectly her handiwork looked. It was the first time she would see her very own work on display. *How exciting!* she thought, but the thought also caused a bit of a nervous tingle to run through her hands. It was only Bastien. He wouldn't judge anything of hers too harshly, so long as it looked good on him.

When Lydia entered the shop, Bastien and Antoinette were arguing passionately about rather bland issues relating to performing. Bastien had set out a mirror and a divider with a few unnecessary accessories beside it and was pointing at the different props dramatically as he tried to explain his point. Lydia couldn't help but giggle at the ridiculous scene.

When she cleared her throat, he jumped a little, then sighed with relief. Shooing Antoinette with a hand, Bastien grabbed Lydia's shoulders and moved her into a chair that looked like a giant pin cushion.

"Let's see it," he said excitedly. Lydia opened the box and handed him each garment, perfectly tailored and embellished. He gasped slightly, then ran his hand along the length of the sleeves with bright eyes. He was at a loss for words, which was a strange and rare occurrence. "You truly have a gift."

Lydia hid her bashful smile. "Go on, then. Try it on."

She watched his silhouette behind the divider. He hung his clothes over the edge and replaced it with the new suit. When he came out to see Lydia, his tie still hung loosely around his neck. Lydia helped him tie it, then turned Bastien towards the mirror and took a step back.

"Well? What do you think?"

He spun around, playing with the long suit jacket and cuffs.

"Lydia Mayler! You have outdone yourself." He grabbed her cheeks and kissed her forehead kindly. "It's perfect."

Antoinette chimed in, "Bastien, you've never looked better! Which, I suppose isn't *that* grand of a compliment."

"Oh, Antoinette. So kind." She stuck her tongue out at him when he wasn't looking. "I love it, Lydia."

"Good to hear." Lydia fixed the edge of his collar.

"What about yours?"

"Almost done," she said, "I just need to put on the final touches. When did Mr. Miller say he could show us around the ballroom he knows of?"

Bastien shrugged. "I haven't the slightest idea. He hasn't reappeared since last night. I've known him for years, and quite frankly I'm sure I remember more about him than he does."

"Oh, well. I'm sure he means well. He *does* know of somewhere we can go, right? To dance, I mean."

"Too many of them, actually. The real wonder is *which*."

"I used to dance in the most lovely ballrooms," Antoinette sighed. "I wish I could come with you."

Bastien patted Antoinette's tiny head. "Chin up there, Lady. Your time will come again."

She smiled sadly, but said nothing in return.

"Speaking of dancing, you have a partner to bring with you, right Lydia?"

Lydia raised her brow. "Since when did I need to bring a partner?"

"Well, you can't dance alone. That's rather sad, isn't it?" Antoinette pointed out.

Lydia fiddled with her hands nervously. "That's alright, I'll just dance with Bastien."

"*I'm* going to practice my playing skills. I'll be off duty as a dancer, darling. Besides, I'm sure you have plenty of options to inquire about."

"Not really."

"Nonsense."

"No, I really don't," Lydia said.

Bastien scoffed in disbelief and waved his hands in the air. "A girl your age? With *no* suitors?"

Lydia's cheeks grew red. "Is it a sin to be perfectly comfortable with who I am and not require completion in others?"

Bastien opened his mouth, then promptly closed it. "Fine, but you still need to bring someone. Don't you have a friend around here?"

Lydia thought to herself. "I do, but I don't think he'd be interested in coming."

"Preposterous. Everyone loves a good, old-fashioned ball."

"It's not the ball that worries me," Lydia said. "It's here. This *place*." She gestured to the store around them.

"Why? What's got you worried?" Antoinette asked.

Lydia glanced between the talking mannequin and the feisty ceramic doll.

"I'm not quite sure, actually."

Bastien went behind the panel and put his regular suit back on. It was clear how much he now despised his old one after a taste of the new, but he said nothing about the matter. He folded it back into the box and sat it neatly on a nearby couch.

Lydia began to pack up her things to return home; that is, until the quiet silhouette of Mr. Miller caught her eye. Bastien and Antoinette were now busy trying to stack a variety of things on a sleeping Pippin, too distracted to notice anything else. Lydia sauntered over to his side, careful not to raise his suspicions. Mr. Miller was taping a reminder for new tea on the side of the cabinet.

"You put that paper up upside down," Lydia pointed out. Sure enough, the note he made to himself was hanging the wrong way.

He half-chuckled. "Dear, me. How silly." He turned it back and stuck the pin into the other side. Ruffling his hair, he began frantically writing something on a piece of used parchment beside the jar filled with Pecuflos and Verunda. She quietly leaned against the desk. Bastien's advice to stay quiet echoed in her head, but she disregarded it.

"I hope you don't mind me asking," she said in a quiet tone, "But are you alright? And please don't lie. I can tell."

He glanced up at her with a somewhat amused face, but the expression fell quickly.

"Lydia I must tell you that I *have* lied once," he said. When he spoke, it wasn't sad or condescending, but a generally normal tone. No hint of anything other than normalcy. Lydia's heart fell, but she retained her calm persona and listened. "I once told you I enjoyed Brightmeadow because it was a nice change to an adventurous life. But that's not really the truth." He paused. "I think I've been so worried about living my life perfectly, I haven't ever really begun living after all."

Lydia chucked internally about the irony of their situation. Two people, so incredibly alike, yet completely opposite. There was Lydia, who feared her life would never begin, and then Mr. Miller, who feared that one day it would.

"What frightens you?"

"Moving on."

He said this in such a way it hardly occurred to Lydia he was hurting. It was the same charismatic voice as always, perhaps only a little bit lower. He hid from the world, and most likely himself.

"Well, of course it does," she finally said. "Moving on frightens everyone with a true heart. But we often find who we truly are when fear plays its hand."

He smiled a little. "You're wise for your age. I wish I could say the same."

She shrugged, but didn't hide her small grin. "I'm only telling you the truth. Besides, I know you, and I know you aren't frightened of anything."

His smile lost him. "Then you don't really know me."

10

The sky held dark clouds and the promise of rain. The whole town seemed to be under some kind of depressive spell with the bleak, muggy air. Hardly anyone made their way about town. A few people wandered into stores, but it was a day to stay at home for most people. The flowers in the shop did not take well to the sharp air, which worried Mrs. Mayler, but Lydia assured her that it would be alright. Besides, unless an even grander flower shop opened, they would never lose business, and no one dared to compete with Mrs. Mayler's success.

Lydia begrudgingly covered the shop for her mother in the morning. Time felt like molasses, drudging slowly in a thick loop. Even people in the street moved with a slow grogginess. Though the sky was gray, the rain refused to fall.

While Lydia hunched over the counter with a bored expression, she watched the people wander back and forth outside the window when

Cedric caught her eye. He was carrying a load of shoeboxes clumsily in his arms. Suddenly, Bastien's reminder of finding someone to bring along to their little ball nudged her memory. Lydia excused herself through a crowd of customers and hurried to greet Cedric with a demeanor much too cheery for the state of the afternoon. Startled, he almost dropped his boxes, but gathered himself together just in time.

"Lydia! Hello, there." His voice sounded very flustered, as if Lydia had just caught him doing something embarrassing. She realized at once that it was very stupid of her to think Cedric would come with her to Mr. Miller's shop. How on earth could she possibly be able to convince him? Perhaps a cover up—yes, a cover up plan would be the best option. Did she *want* to lie to Cedric? No, but she knew there was no other way for him to consider coming along with her. Besides, she had a good reason for doing it. *She* was helping Bastien, and Cedric would be helping *her* by supporting her artwork. But what cover would be believable enough?

"You know Mrs. Fisher's ball this Friday evening?" *Believable enough*, she thought.

Cedric tilted his head with a confused smile. "What about it?"

"You should come with me. We can drink all of her champagne and steal her biscuits."

Cedric laughed, then caught his boxes falling from him once more. "*Us?* Going to Mrs. Fisher's ball? Did you even get invited?"

Lydia rolled her eyes. "I don't go if I don't have an invitation." *That* wasn't a lie. She *wouldn't* go without an invitation, and she never *said* she got one. "Come on, it'll be loads of fun."

Cedric thought to himself, then gave in. "Alright. I'll do it."

"Perfect!" Lydia clapped her hands then made her way back up the shop door. "Meet me here at eight o'clock Friday. And wear something nice."

He chuckled and waved goodbye with his foot, then continued down Magnolia Lane. Lydia smiled and silently cheered to herself. The perfect plan! And, if Lydia knew Cedric, he wouldn't back out when he realized they were a long way from Mrs. Fisher's, so long as he was right by Lydia's side.

* * *

After lunch she managed to sneak away down Dandelion Lane and into the shop. Mr. Miller was hunched over the jar while Bastien kept trying to move a curious Pippin away with his foot.

"Good afternoon, everyone." Lydia shut the door behind her and removed her hat with a sigh. "Please tell me we're doing something interesting today."

Mr. Miller chuckled. "If I'm thinking correctly, then yes. We are." He paused for a moment and fiddled with the jar. "Though I'm hopeful I'm incorrect."

Lydia furrowed her brow. "Anywhere's better than here. What's got you worried?"

"You know," he said, "Not everywhere is as *safe* as Brightmeadow."

"And? Nowhere is as *boring* as Brightmeadow, either."

Bastien made an agreeing face to Mr. Miller.

"See?"

Mr. Miller shrugged Bastien away jokingly. He reached into his pocket and pulled out an old advertisement with large black lettering.

W.E.'s Emporium of Magical (and other) Services
Registered Wizards and Witches Only
Rolling Hills, 672 Dark Cove
Keep Quiet.

"I found this pamphlet from an old collection of mine. 'Across Rolling Hills' is what the spell said. I assume it's referring to Rolling Hills, a town known for their. . .*unique* charm."

"Charm?" Pippin tried to jump up onto the table to join the conversation, but was promptly dismissed by Bastien's hand. Mr. Miller glared at him. Sighing, Bastien scooted over enough for Pippin to be included.

"You'll see for yourselves. Maybe. Quite honestly, I'm debating on whether or not to bring you at all." Simultaneously, Bastien and Lydia protested with loud voices. Mr. Miller groaned and covered his ears, but the two persisted until he gave up and threw his hands in the air.

"Fine. You can come with. As long as you promise *never* to leave my side."

The two complied, but neither took his request seriously.

"Take these." He took two black cloaks from a nearby rack and handed one to Lydia and Bastien. Pippin received a mini sized one. He smiled brightly. Mr. Miller tied his around his shoulders nervously. Though chipper, Lydia sensed a tinge of anxiety in his demeanor. He was fixing his hair about twice as often as usual, and every time he did so, his hands fidgeted even more.

When they all stepped outside, Lydia pulled the cloak around her tighter to shield herself from the sharp air. The dragonfly buzzed patiently on the ground as they climbed into the seats. Pippin held onto Lydia's leg (slightly less frightened this time) as they flew off into distant grey clouds and a dim horizon.

After a good bit of flying through cold air, Mr. Miller landed on top of a grassy hill a little ways out from a dark town. From where they stood, Lydia could see grand amounts of smoke drifting up from old buildings. The whole town felt gloomy, with stone streets leading them into a quiet, grim atmosphere. People sauntered through the streets with heads hanging down, gripping each other for warmth and safety. A group of cloaked figures sporting plague masks marched by Lydia. She gasped quietly and moved closer to Bastien. Pippin gulped and hid under Mr. Miller's cloak.

"Stay close," he murmured.

They traveled farther into the town, passing by ominous shops and sad looking people. Lydia tried to keep her head down, but she couldn't help but look around at the filth and misery of it all. Suddenly, Brightmeadow seemed very pleasant to her. She now understood what Mr. Miller meant now when he said Brightmeadow was a nice change to his life. With that said, she still believed it was beyond boring. Nevertheless, she now supposed it was a rather good place to call home.

Mr. Miller brought them to a corner with a small shop snug in the shadows. Looking over his shoulder, he cracked open the door and ushered them inside, closing the door swiftly behind him.

It smelled of cobwebs and mold. A hint of tobacco and faded pages of old, forgotten books lingered through the air. Everything looked either to be brown, black, or grey. Empty bird cages, leather books damaged with water, weird skeletal hands in glass display boxes, and other strange items took up every inch of the shop. You could hardly walk through the narrow aisle without tripping over some weird bear trap. Beetles, butterflies, and bugs were on display in glass cases, and on a far wall, an assortment of glasses held objects in goo that Lydia really didn't want to know the identity of. Mr. Miller didn't seem the slightest bit fazed.

Bastien grabbed a funky looking cane with a crow's head and jumped out of a corner to scare Pippin. He shrieked, then ran and hid under Mr. Miller's cloak again. Bastien laughed, but Mr. Miller did not find it so funny. However, when he turned away from Bastien, Lydia noticed him trying to suppress a subtle grin.

Lydia perused the crammed shelves on one side of the wall. Dozens of shabbily labeled jars contained varieties of strange powders and liquids. Lydia dared not touch the bubbling or smoking ones. One of the bottles stood away from the others, untouched by mold and other residue. Lydia wiped the dust away from the label:

Necare

User Beware.

"Lydia, don't touch that!" Mr. Miller snatched it from her and carefully put it back in the cupboard.

"Sorry," she muttered.

"That's poison; it could kill you in an instant." He shooed her away from the mess and back over to the front counter where Pippin trembled by Bastien's side.

On a counter overloaded with the strangest of items, a silver bell balanced on top of a bone that could be human, but Lydia couldn't tell. Mr. Miller rung the bell and waited expectantly.

From seemingly nowhere, a ghastly looking lady drudged herself to the counter with a gloomy expression. Her skin was pale white with deep cheekbones and a prominent collar bone. She was incredibly thin and sickly. Though rather short, black slip shoes lifted her off the ground a few inches and complemented her tulle dress and dirty, ripped tights. Wild black hair was arranged into some sort of a half updo, but most of it fell raggedy down her back. Her eyes were grim. A shiver went down Lydia's spine.

The woman barely looked at Mr. Miller when he greeted her. "Good afternoon. I was hoping to inquire about a purchase. My name is —"

"I know who you are." She spoke matter-of-factly. She shifted a pair of goggles off her forehead and tossed them aside.

Mr. Miller appeared taken aback. He cleared his throat and furrowed his brow. "How's that?"

She smiled slyly. Incredibly subtle, but Lydia noticed it in a flicker of a second. "I've heard loads about you. Years and years ago that is, but I could never mistake what I once heard."

He shifted uncomfortably. "Heard from who?"

She leaned under the counter and pulled out a dusty box. Opening it up, she took out a large metal spider and walked around from the counter and out into the store, looking for a place to put it. "I knew Laurie. Way back when."

Mr. Miller's face fell and grew whiter than the woman's at once. He tried to say something, but he couldn't quite find the words. Lydia glanced towards Bastien for validation in her confusion, but Bastien seemed to know exactly what the lady meant. It seemed that Lydia was the only person in the world who hadn't the slightest idea of who Laurie was. Bastien put a hand on Mr. Miller's shoulder to calm him, which did exactly that.

"I'm Wither." She placed the spider in a cracked glass case. "I've always wondered if you'd ever stop by."

"How do you know Laurie?" He asked.

"Who's Laurie?" Lydia whispered to Bastien. He quickly shook his head *no* and motioned for her to be quiet.

"I *did* know her." Wither hummed to herself and wiped some dust from the tabletops with a melancholy look. Mr. Miller followed her over to the counter where she slouched on a chair. "Vincent, isn't it?"

"I prefer Hugo."

She chuckled to herself. "Of course. I forgot." Bastien watched Mr. Miller worriedly. Lydia took notice. "You came here for something."

"Oh, yes." Mr. Miller cleared his throat and handed her a stained pamphlet. "I found this in my shop. You see, my friend Bastien here is under a curse, and we need to finish a spell so we can find the witch who cursed him and convince her to break it."

Wither took the paper from him and nodded. "I sensed some form of energy when you walked in. It's been a while hasn't it?"

Bastien sighed. "Years."

153

She pursed her lips and thought for a moment, then said, "Come with me." She disappeared into a door behind the counter, leaving the group in a tense silence. Lydia had a compulsion to ask Mr. Miller about the unknown party, but Bastien must have realized she was about to ask and promptly shook his head as a warning. Though curious, she complied. Hesitantly, Mr. Miller motioned for the group to follow the strange woman through the door and behind a black, velvet curtain.

The room smelled strongly of incense and burnt wood. Carpets and mismatched drapes covered the dimly lit walls and surrounded a table with three chairs on one side and an empty space on the other. Candles were the only provider of light. A stack of black, matte cards shuffled in the middle of the table. Lydia fought the urge to cough away the dust and ripe scent of sage. Wither motioned them into the seats and stood hunched over on the other side of the table.

The woman revealed a small vial with swirling green dust. She sat it on the table and raised an eyebrow at Mr. Miller like he already knew what it was. He stared blankly.

"With a spell such as the one you're trying to accomplish Vincent—"

"Hugo."

"—right, *Hugo*, strong emotions are tied within it, which means strong emotions must be used to complete it. I'm assuming the other components have contained old and harmful memories?"

He nodded.

"You need one more truth to it." She held the glass in the air and watched the swirling dust with wide eyes. "Fear."

He squinted. "How is that to be accomplished?"

"This dust will contain your fears within it. Once this potion is complete, we may continue with our—" she cleared her throat. "—ritual. So tell me, Hugo . . . " She held the glass closely to his lips and leaned in closely. "What is it that you fear?"

Lydia had an idea. He did, in fact, tell her what he feared in the first place, but she held the concern that more would be revealed than he desired. He didn't reply.

Wither raised her eyebrow. "Go on."

"It's not that easy," he replied sternly.

"How could it be that hard?"

With a sigh, he bit the inside of his lip. Lydia could tell he was becoming agitated. Pippin shifted towards Lydia.

"Tell me." Wither crept out from behind the wood that separated them and circled Mr. Miller, holding the vial up closely to his face. Lydia and the others backed away from the two of them. Bastien's hands fidgeted at his side, ready to defend his friend at the slightest disturbance. Mr. Miller shook his head with refusal.

Wither scoffed lightly. "Fine. Then we'll do things *my* way."

At once, the cards flung from the table with a flurry of charcoal dust. Lydia shielded her eyes and coughed. When she opened her eyes again, she was surrounded by blackness and a strange echo of something she couldn't quite place. A voice, it sounded like.

"Mr. Miller?" She called.

No answer.

"Bastien?"

No answer.

"Oh, don't worry, dear," the voice of Wither echoed around her. "He always seems to find his way to those who need him."

At once, Mr. Miller appeared into her sight. He breathed a sigh of relief and began to run towards her.

"Well, not *always*."

And just before he reached Lydia, he vanished once more.

Lydia's breath caught in her throat. "What do you want?"

Almost as if on cue, the blackness faded away. Relieved, she caught her breath, but her relief was short-lived. Four large tarot cards formed around her in a tall tower, but the images were hidden from her sight in darkness. She gasped and backed away, but her back hit another. She covered her mouth and whirled around to Mr. Miller. The cards blocked them in.

"I know, I know, you hate the search of future, Vincent," Wither's voice echoed, "But why don't we look at the present?"

In an instant, a light illuminated one of the cards: a man with a robe holding a lantern with a six-pointed star, but he was flipped upside-down.

The light hit the second card: a picture of a jester juggling something, also upside-down.

The third light flickered: the image of a magician with objects representing each of the elements came into view. The card flipped upside-down.

The last card revealed its prophecy: a priestess standing between two pillars, upside-down just like all the rest.

"I'll ask you again, Vincent." The cards flipped away and shuffled around them. The noise was overwhelming, like water full of lead running off the edge of a rocky cliff. Shots being fired over and over and over—it never ceased. Lydia and Mr. Miller covered their ears with shaky hands, trying desperately to block out the endless noise of taunting, shuffling, cards. Then, just as quickly as it began, the cards disappeared, leaving the two in an infinite darkness. A single candle lit in the distance, illuminating a worn, dusty mirror.

"What are you afraid of?"

Mr. Miller approached the mirror slowly, never breaking his eye contact with the two eyes that stared back at him. The muffled sound of shouting caught Lydia's attention. She turned around and saw Bastien trapped behind a window of glass, pleading for Mr. Miller not to approach the mirror. Lydia's heart sank. She tried to scream, but no sound escaped. She tried to run, but suddenly her legs wouldn't work. She tried to reach out, but a window of glass blocked her from going any farther.

"Mr. Miller!" She banged on the glass, but it was no use. He was already right in front of the mirror, its sides chipped with age and the candle flickering with smoke. He didn't move an inch. He just stood there with vacant eyes, arms like anvils on either side of him. Lydia noticed a shadow place a hand on his shoulder behind him and whisper something in his ear. He barely reacted.

A few specks of glittering dust in the corner of the glass caught Lydia's eye—the same shimmering powder Wither blew through the cards earlier. Though Lydia knew that it was most likely a horrible idea, she bent down and blew the dust onto the window. For a moment, her eyes tingled, but when she opened them, the glass disappeared. She crept towards the mirror under the cover of darkness.

She couldn't understand what the shadow was saying. It sounded like shallow promises and memories. When she saw Mr. Miller's face, though, she wasn't sure who was speaking to him: Wither or himself. The shadow caught her eye and disappeared with a hiss. The candle blew out and left a trail of smoke dancing through the air.

It was quiet for a moment. Lydia at last spoke. "Are you alright?"

The floor fell out from under them, sending them spiraling down a dark hole of twisting curves. Cards flew in and out between them, their faces laughing and shrieking in the pictures. Lydia reached out to grab one, but the sword of a knight stuck out from his card and cut the edge of her hand.

"Lydia!" Mr. Miller called through the dim light of falling candles. He reached his arm out to her. Just when she tried to grab hold of it, the falling ceased and they hit the ground, padded with dead leaves and wilted flower petals. Lydia gasped shallowly, unable to move due to her body numb with fear. Mr. Miller climbed shakily to his feet, wading through the dead plants clumsily. His legs sank through all the way to his knee.

"Enough, Wither!" He looked up and around, but saw nothing. He glanced towards Lydia, then hung his head low and sighed with defeat. "Fine." He opened his arms up in an act of giving in. "You win. You can have whatever you want from me." He swallowed hard. "Just don't mess with them anymore. Please."

For a moment, nothing happened. Lydia began to climb to her feet, but ducked back down into the leaves when the figure of Wither appeared in the distance. She held a lantern out in front of her to illuminate her path. She walked on top of green, vibrant leaves and colorful flowers, but at the passing of her presence, they promptly shriveled up and decayed.

"Isn't it ironic?" She said to Mr. Miller. "A witch, whom nature has rejected?" She bent down and picked up the single remaining rose. It crumbled in her hands. "I can't remember the last time I got to hold a rose." Mr. Miller didn't reply. Wither watched him carefully. "You really love them, don't you?"

He said nothing.

Wither squinted, as if to find a flaw in his eyes. She didn't find what she was looking for. Then, much to Lydia's surprise, she smiled. It was soft. Delicate. Unlike anything she would've expected from someone like Wither.

She took the vial from her pocket and uncorked it. Mr. Miller glanced at it fearfully. Wither stepped closer.

After a sigh of dread, Mr. Miller closed his eyes and leaned into the smoke overflowing from the vial and whispered something into it. Wither held it to his cheek and captured a single tear. He stepped back and observed Wither as she corked the vial and held it in her hand.

"Is there anything more terrifying?"

Then, in an instant, they were all back in the Emporium.

Pippin fainted into Bastien's arms when he saw Lydia and Mr. Miller. Though in any other context it would've been hilarious, Bastien knew it was not the time to be laughing. Mr. Miller half-smiled to him, then turned to Wither.

She presented the vial (now grey and heavy) to Mr. Miller. He took it from her cold hands in exchange for a small bag of bronze and silver coins. She hesitated, as if at once she felt guilty, but took it anyways and slid it into the desk drawer of her workspace.

"Just so you know," she spoke lowly, "She was scared you would forget her one day." His eyes raised to the grim woman who now all of a sudden seemed gentle. "It's nice to see that even beyond her years, her greatest fear still hasn't caught her." She paused. "I wish I could say the same for you."

Mr. Miller nodded shortly, but said nothing in response. He bowed his head to acknowledge a goodbye, then ushered the group out of the store.

They left in a daze. The second they stepped out, Mr. Miller doubled over to catch his breath, which had left him long ago. Bastien immediately went to his side to make sure he was alright. Mr. Miller brushed him off and assured him he was fine, but none of them really believed it. He straightened himself back up and, much to their surprise, laughed.

"My, what a strange woman," he said. "I liked her."

"Hey!" A voice boomed from across the square. A large man with long, raggedy hair and tattered clothes pointed accusingly. "Vincent Miller, I won't let you get away again, you son of a—"

"Oh, dear," Mr. Miller gulped as the man began to charge them. "Now would probably be a good time to run."

Scooping a terrified Pippin into his arms, Mr. Miller bolted in the opposite direction to where the hills outside of the city rolled. Lydia and Bastien followed close behind. She glanced back and saw a whole crew of cloaked figures chasing them.

"Come on, now!" Mr. Miller exclaimed, smiling slightly as if it were an exciting time.

"Why's he after you?" Lydia panted as she sprinted beside him.

"I may have taken something from him years ago."

"So you *are* a thief!" Lydia exclaimed in shock.

"No! Of course not!" He shushed a trembling Pippin. "He stole it first."

They ran the length of the town, toppling over small carts and almost tripping over stones and stray wheels. The group began to catch up to them, but Mr. Miller was faster and smarter. After a single turn to the left, the hills welcomed them and a clear view of the dragonfly came into sight.

"Just a bit farther, everyone!" Mr. Miller called. He was right. About thirty seconds later, they were all onboard, not even buckled in when Mr. Miller yanked the wheel up and out of sight. Unfortunately, in her panic, Lydia had not yet caught her footing and fell back into the grass. Mr. Miller was already in the distance, but by the worried shrieking, she knew she wasn't forgotten. She could hear Bastien screaming *run!*, which wasn't really necessary because she figured that was rather obvious.

The hooded figures had gained distance on her. Mr. Miller had to keep that dragonfly going, but managed to slow it just enough for her to catch up. A ravine approached quickly ahead.

Mr. Miller's hair whipped furiously in the wind as he called back to her. "Hurry, Laurie!"

"Laurie?" Lydia stumbled, then caught herself just in time. Mr. Miller didn't even notice, but Bastien certainly did.

Lydia grunted and forced herself to go faster. She was only a few meters away from the dragonfly now. Three meters. Two meters. One meter. She was close enough to jump in.

"Come on, Lydia!" Bastien reached his hand as far as it would go. "I've got you!"

The chasers were right on her heels. Lydia pushed forward more, her lungs catching fire with each breath she inhaled. It felt as if each gasp inhaled cold icicles that pierced her lungs and punched her heart over and over. She reached her hand out, then pushed it forward even more. Just a bit closer. . .a few more inches. . .

The edge of a cliff approached quickly. If she didn't grab his hand now, she'd be a goner. With an overwhelming (and, frankly ridiculous) amount of faith in herself, she leapt hard off a rock and pushed the air, gripping her hand tightly around Bastien's arm. He exclaimed a shout of relief as they watched the chasers fade away angrily in the distance.

Bastien and Pippin managed to pull Lydia onto the dragonfly with a great tug. She turned over on her back and stared up at the sky as she caught her breath and her bearings. The wind blew away the perspiration on her forehead, but only made the burning grow deeper in her lungs.

"Are you alright?" Bastien leaned over her worriedly.

She gave a weak thumbs up. "Perfectly swell."

"Good. Oh, dear, I think you made my heart stop!"

"I think mine did, too," she panted.

Her lungs were not satisfied until they reached the ground in Brightmeadow.

11

Friday night approached much quicker than Lydia anticipated. After staying up much too late to perfect the designs on her dress, she was finally happy with the result and quite proud of the handiwork.

She placed the dress in a velvet box and managed to sneak downstairs and out through the front door. The rest of the family (including Rosie) remained distracted in Henry's room, making sure all of his new clothes were put up properly. Lydia told her parents she would be with Cedric on a night picnic. That was honestly a very stupid cover up, but as long as Cedric was involved, they trusted her. She snuck out in her normal clothes as to not raise suspicion if they happened to wander out and see her leaving. She would have to change back into the normal clothes before she returned home, but that wasn't her worry at the moment.

The streets were dark and slightly chilly as Lydia awaited Cedric's presence. At last, his shadow appeared under a streetlight. He wore a very nice black suit (Lydia assumed it was his father's) and his hair was slicked back handsomely. He smiled nervously.

"You look wonderful, Cedric."

"You as well," he said with a tad bit of confusion. "I hope you don't take this the wrong way, but are you really wearing *that* to Mrs. Fisher's?"

Lydia chuckled to herself and held up the velvet box. "Don't worry. I'm changing."

"Off to Mrs. Fisher's then." He said excitedly, starting down the empty street. "You know, I've always wanted to go to one of her balls. Just to see what it's like, you know?"

"I do." Lydia's plan was unfolding perfectly. "Oh—oh, no!"

"What? What's wrong?"

"I think I misplaced my pocket book. . .I can't find it, I could've *sworn* I had it here with me."

"Well, where do you remember having it?"

She hadn't lost her pocket book of course, but if she said she happened to go into a shop at the edge of Dandelion Lane and sit outside reading a book during the afternoon, that would be enough to convince Cedric to go and investigate further.

"Let's see. . .I purchased a book in that book store at the end of Dandelion Lane and read outside for the rest of the afternoon. That's the last I remember of it."

He smiled as if he suddenly came up with a good idea. "Well, why don't we go look and see if it's there?"

"Good idea," Lydia replied. Earlier, she had left an empty pocketbook in the outside windowsill of the store, which was right across from Mr. Miller's shop.

When they reached the window, Lydia pretended to act relieved to see the pocket book sitting right where she had placed it. Cedric looked very pleased as well.

"You know," Lydia said, wandering towards Mr. Miller's shop, "Why don't we go in here for a bit? It *is* a night of adventure. Why not just take a look around?" Cedric tried to protest, but Lydia was already in the door before he could say no. With a flustered sigh, he followed in after her.

The store was lit dimly with antique lights and candles. The smell of dozens of varying scents was a little overwhelming, but it was much better than the usual. Just as Lydia had begged Bastien, he had cleaned it up just enough not to cause a nervous attack to any newcomer. Antoinette, upset about her exclusion (as usual), pouted in the back of the store and refused to speak to anyone. Pippin was told to remain in the back until Cedric was accustomed to the rest of the chaos.

"Lydia! Welcome back." Bastien greeted her with a kiss on either cheek. "And you must be Cedric. So lovely to meet you, at last."

Cedric froze in shock. Sometimes Lydia forgot that Bastien was a talking mannequin, and it hardly occurred to her that he would most likely frighten Cedric.

"T-thank you," he gulped, then murmured to Lydia, "Were they expecting us?"

"Of course we were," Mr. Miller interrupted. "You *are* seeking a ball, aren't you?"

Cedric tried to speak, but no words came out.

"Oh, excuse my manners. I'm Mr. Miller, but you can call me Hugo." He shook Cedric's limp hand. "Pleased to meet you."

"And. . .you. *You're* Mr. Miller?"

"I should hope so," he replied, "Or we'd have a real problem on our hands. Come along now to the ballroom. I assure you it's wonderful."

Lydia started to follow him, but Cedric pulled her back. "Lydia. A word please?" She agreed and listened to him with a tilt of her head. "I thought we were going to Mrs. Fisher's. And. . .why are they so. . ." He paused for a moment, then hung his head when it all came together for him. "We were coming here all along, weren't we?"

"I'm sorry, Cedric, I should've told you, but I didn't want you to freak out," Lydia admitted. "I promised Bastien that I would find a way for him to practice playing so that we *could* go to Mrs. Fisher's ball. Please don't be angry with me."

Cedric looked deep into her eyes and suddenly his worry subsided. He relented with a stubborn sigh. "Alright, fine. But that doesn't mean I'm not the *slightest* bit annoyed by all this."

"Thank you." She hugged him tightly. He didn't seem to want to let go.

Mr. Miller revealed a door with intricate golden trim and a pretty door handle. They all entered into a nice foyer with gold embellished walls and painted ceilings. Lydia informed Cedric, Bastien, and a now present Pippin to go to the ballroom and wait for her. Cedric, though clearly not a fan of being alone with the two of them, didn't argue (he *did* handle the talking frog much better than Lydia had expected him to). She found an empty room with a mirror and donned the dress, being careful to not rip or be too rough with it. She finished tying the corset in the back and placed the golden strings in her hair. She knew it was rather conceited, but she couldn't help but admire herself in the mirror.

Mr. Miller smiled when she came back out into the foyer. "Fantastic job, Lydia. It looks perfect."

"Thank you. My hands could sure use a break, though," she laughed. On a small table beside him, Lydia noticed the spell jar with Zabuli's parchment. "Why's that here? I thought we had all of the elements."

He groaned. "I thought we did, too, but it isn't working. I don't know why. I figured while you were all in there I would stay out here in the quiet to work it out."

"Could it be that we're missing something?"

"I have all of the clues here, but I don't understand *why* it isn't working. Did I just misinterpret the spell, or am I completely thoughtless? I must be missing something. . .but what?"

"Lydia!" Bastien called from the other room. "We're ready!"

She glanced at Mr. Miller, who was staring wide-eyed at the wall as if a sudden grand idea had crossed his mind.

"It'll be alright. We'll figure it out," Lydia assured.

He nodded, yet still retained that strange observant look in his eye. "Eventually. Until that dearest moment, go have fun. You deserve it."

Lydia smiled, then gathered up her skirts and pushed the golden doors open. She greeted a grand ballroom with dazzling chandeliers made of golden flowers and jewels. Cedric stood in the middle of the shining floor, marveling at the grandeur ballroom, but when his eyes landed on Lydia, it was clear he saw her as more beautiful than any of the finest gold around them. Lydia didn't seem to notice the deep wonder in his eyes, though—only the glimmering elegance of a ballroom that would humiliate Mrs. Fisher. She chuckled at the thought.

Down the stairs she went, holding on to the railing and her dress, praying she didn't fall. Bastien rosined up his bow and gave a short bow to Lydia. Pippin stumbled beside him awkwardly.

"Lydia Mayler, you look positively stunning." Bastien said. "And I must say, I do believe I look quite lovely as well."

"I'd be lying if I said anything against it." She smiled. Lydia looked down at Pippin, who stared at her with a starlit gaze in his eyes.

"Hello, Pippin. Everything alright?"

He nodded in a daze. Lydia giggled. Cedric waited for her towards the middle of the floor, still very nervous about the whole thing. Lydia didn't understand why. So what if it wasn't Mrs. Fisher's ball? He didn't have to be so scared. Lydia knew he trusted her, so why all of a sudden was he at such a loss for words?

"Hello, Cedric," she said with her charming smile.

"Miss Mayler—Lydia," he stammered. Holding his arm out, Lydia took it, then followed his lead out into the middle of a shining circle of gold on the floor. Bastien strung out a few notes, then gave the motion he and Pippin were ready.

"I must warn you, I don't know what I'm doing," Lydia said.

"Oh, what a relief. Me neither."

He took her by the hand and spun her around once, twice, then again. She really didn't know what to do, so she just laughed and followed Cedric's awkward lead, relieved he was just as clueless. Pippin glared jealously, but there was no denying the kind chuckle that escaped him when Lydia spun and did a little wave in his direction. Cedric, despite having a wonderful time, kept glancing towards Bastien and Pippin nervously, as though they might turn on him at any moment. Neither of the musicians paid him any mind, but it was glaringly obvious to Lydia. She figured he was only being shy, yet the subtlety of his hostility brought Lydia a tinge of discomfort. With grace, she decided to dismiss it.

Lydia smiled at the sudden friendliness between Pippin and Bastien. They harmonized with each other perfectly, and every so often Bastien would nod approvingly to Pippin and his harp.

"What's got you all smiley?" Cedric joked.

She shrugged lightly. "Everything."

He tilted his head to the side and leaned forward a bit. Just as he moved closer, Lydia turned over her shoulder to give Bastien a quick round of applause for a rather difficult measure of music. Bastien smiled, Cedric frowned.

The lights turned the floor to gold. Through the large windows in the ceiling, the night sky peeked through, but the golden light overcame the darkness. It shone off Lydia's hair and dress. The light illuminated Cedric's smile. That is, when he chose to smile. It came and went, just as the tides did at sea. Sometimes vacant, yet mostly generous. She watched him carefully to see if she could pinpoint what caused him trouble, but the closer she looked, the more he seemed to pull away.

They danced for who knows how long until Bastien finally held out one last note with a delicate vibrato.

Lydia clapped and ran over to give him a warm hug, hardly noticing the disappointed look on Cedric's face and the way he held onto her hand until the very last moment she let go. "Bastien, that was wonderful! Mrs. Fisher is going to be blown away by your talent!"

"You really think so?"

"I know so! I've never heard such music," she exclaimed.

Bastien rubbed the back of his head bashfully, but Lydia knew he enjoyed the attention. If Bastien was *anything*, he certainly was dramatic. He didn't fool Lydia for a second.

"Don't act so shy, Bastien," she teased. "The dramatics suit you."

"If you insist." And, before she knew what was happening, Bastien started on a rather difficult piece of music, forgetting that she and Cedric were still there.

Lydia laughed to herself. "That's what normally happens," she told Cedric. "I *would* be annoyed if he wasn't so talented."

Cedric half-chuckled, but Lydia could tell he wasn't as amused. She noticed his nerves return once more with a tilt of the head. What could he possibly be so afraid of?

"Lydia, is it alright if I have a moment to speak with you?"

Lydia, not catching the seriousness of his tone (due to her incredibly happy state), replied, "Of course. What's the matter?"

Cedric fiddled with his hands. "Maybe somewhere. . .a bit more quiet?"

Lydia picked up on his manner and nodded hesitantly. She glanced back at Bastien to try and signal a warning to come help her, but he was too busy showing off to notice. Lydia followed Cedric up the staircase and through a large pair of shimmering glass doors that led to a beautiful balcony overlooking the forest. The trees glistened with silver flowers, and streams of crystal water sparkled in the moonlight.

"How beautiful," Lydia murmured to herself, hardly noticing Cedric's solemn stare. She smiled, then met his gaze.

Her smile faded.

Cedric glanced down at his hands nervously, then back to Lydia. "Lydia, I must ask you something serious."

She nodded, hiding the nerves that suddenly appeared with the statement.

He took a deep breath. "I know we're still young, but it is the custom in our world at this age. We've known each other for so long now—long enough to know most everything about you, and appreciate everything about you." He paused. Lydia was still trying to figure out where exactly he was going with this. "I suppose what I'm trying to say is that I care about you. *Deeply* care about you." Suddenly, Lydia knew what was about to happen, and she also knew that she was not in the slightest bit prepared for it. "When the time is right in the coming year, Lydia, would you do me the honor of—marrying me?"

Lydia's breath caught in her throat. She fought the urge to choke. Cedric watched her with expectant, hopeful eyes, but she had no words. Nothing! She couldn't even think. All of a sudden, their years of friendship were *gone*. Lydia only had the choice to abolish it in one of two ways: she could say yes, which would then disregard their relationship as friends and move to a romantic relationship (which Lydia *certainly* wasn't ready for), or she could say no, and lose Cedric completely.

"Please, just say something," he said with a hint of dread.

"Cedric, I. . ." Lydia bit the inside of her lip and sighed. "You know I care about you too, but just. . .not like that." Lydia could instantly see the sorrow in his eyes. "I'm sorry, but it's just all too much." She spoke carefully, leaving frustration out of her tone. "I can't marry you, Cedric. I just can't."

"Why not?" He wasn't angry. Just sad. This question didn't offend Lydia. She understood. And, given their history, she was okay to offer an explanation. That was, until, he added: "I only want to protect you."

"Protect me?" Lydia scoffed. "First of all, protect me from *what*? And second of all, in the nicest way I can say this, it isn't your *job* to protect me."

"Come on, Lydia. Open your eyes. What are you doing here? What are *we* doing here? We're in a ballroom with a talking mannequin from some weird shop that I didn't even want to go to in the first place! This isn't like you."

"Isn't *like* me? Cedric, I can think of nothing more perfect to complement who I am, and I must say I don't think you really know me at *all*."

Cedric squeezed the bridge of his nose. "Lydia. You've been obsessing over this place. You've gone to that shop *everyday* for the past who knows how long, and you think all of these *people* are your best friends."

"They *are* my friends!" She interjected, stamping her foot down and silencing him. "And I thought you were, too."

He rubbed his face in frustration. "How could you not have known, Lydia? The past eight years, how did you not realize?"

"Realize *what*, Cedric?"

He finally exploded and threw his hands in the air. "That I am completely and utterly in love with you!"

Lydia fell silent and stared at him with a certain kind of horror. In *love* with her? It was a concept Lydia could not understand, nor did she *want* to understand. She looked down, then out over the edge of the rails and towards the shining moon. He sighed, then ran his hands through his hair and leaned against the rails. Lydia tried to say something.

"Cedric—"

"Please." He held his hand up and shook his head. "Please just don't."

He left, not in a hurry. Lydia heard the glass doors open, then close harshly. The sound made her jump, but she remained frozen in shock, staring and staring at the fading horizon.

And in an instant, eight years of friendship were gone.

It was as if they never even existed. They drifted off into the cold wind of the night and disappeared. Lydia no longer knew Cedric which, amidst all the strange things occurring around them, was the hardest thing to understand.

The door behind her flung open. Lydia spun around, hoping to see an apologetic Cedric, but it was Mr. Miller in a frenzied state.

"I think I figured it out," he exclaimed. "*Zabuli*. I think I know where she is."

Lydia, of course, was excited with this news, but she couldn't bring herself to show it, for her heart still hung heavy with the loss of her dearest friend. She mustered up every ounce of enthusiasm she could.

"Really? Where?"

He paused, as if hesitant to tell her.

"Where, Mr. Miller?"

He bit the inside of his lip and vacillated:

"Brightmeadow."

12

"I don't understand," Bastien exclaimed, "Brightmeadow! This whole time. . ."

Mr. Miller held the jar in front of him and watched it curiously. "How clever of her. The last place we would've ever thought to look. But where could she be?"

"Wait a moment," Lydia said. "Mr. Miller, didn't you say witches often refer to themselves with pseudonyms?" He nodded. "That means she could be anybody! She could work in a shop, or live down the road from me, or—"

She stopped, with the sudden realization that she should've known from the very beginning.

"What? What is it?" Mr. Miller leaned forward.

"It's Mrs. Fisher." She paused for a moment and sat back in her chair to gain her bearings. "Mrs. Fisher is Zabuli."

"How could that be?" Bastien half scoffed.

Lydia jumped back to her feet. "Well, we all know how *inviting* she is. I mean, she hosts parties every week. And you *did* say, Mr. Miller, that witches live among nature and often claim it as their own? Mrs. Fisher lives right on the sea in an *enormous* mansion, which *could* count as her castle! And what if all of her 'gold and wealth' is really just—"

"Golden dust!" They said at the same time.

"I think you're right," Mr. Miller said. "Lydia, do you know how we can get to her? As inconspicuously as possible?"

She thought to herself, going through a number of scenarios in her head. She couldn't just wander around town until she found her. That would be too odd and strange. Besides, the longer Lydia spent looking for her, the more suspicious that would be. By then, Mrs. Fisher could possibly be onto her and figure out her plot. She also couldn't ask around. That would raise suspicions as well. Lydia needed to speak to her as privately as possible.

"I've got it," Lydia said. "I'll go to her house on Dahlia Road and ask if she needs to order new bouquets. Every time she has a party she stops by the shop to order a load of flowers, but she hasn't been by this week. I'll ask if she wants to place an order, and while we're there, you two can sneak in and figure out where she keeps her golden dust. Then, we can convince her to break the spell!"

"Brilliant!" Bastien exclaimed. "But can you be sure that it'll work?"

"I don't know," Lydia replied. "But it's the best we've got."

"Well, it's good enough for me." Bastien looked at Mr. Miller hopefully. He smiled back, but only showed his worried persona to Lydia.

Mr. Miller pulled her aside and spoke seriously. "Are you sure about this? Evil can be a lot more dangerous than you think, and I don't know if I can have something happen to you again."

"Again?" Lydia furrowed her brow. "I don't think anything's happened to me before."

He moved back a bit as if he had just come to a realization about something, then shook his head to himself and cleared his throat. "Sorry. I don't know what I was thinking."

"That's alright. Don't worry. I promise I'll be fine." Lydia smiled warmly. "Besides, Mrs. Fisher would never harm me. If anyone in town found out, she would be a goner."

"I suppose so."

A nervous silence fell between them, but neither wanted to point out the tension in the room. Lydia excused herself to change back into her normal clothes, then said her goodnights.

"I'll be back tomorrow," she promised.

"Rest until then," Mr. Miller said. "You'll need it."

***

That night as Lydia walked home, she had never felt so unreal. Numb. Zabuli had been right under their noses this whole time. For *years*. Mr. Miller protested her walking home alone, but Lydia assured him she would be okay. Truthfully, she wasn't okay, but she needed the time to be alone to think. It was only a matter of time until she was alone again. Cedric would be gone before she knew it, and when Bastien became human again, he and Mr. Miller would surely travel to the places they were meant to be. Lydia would be alone, with only a dim hope for her future.

After the whole fiasco at the ballroom, she couldn't find where Cedric fled after he left. This worried Lydia, but she tried her best not to think about it. Cedric would end up talking to her again. Eventually. He had to. Right?

The sky was almost completely dark. The air held a crisp breeze that sent a chill down Lydia's spine, though she wasn't sure if that was a clue to be fearful of something else.

The door was slightly ajar, which was unusual for this hour of night. She creaked the door open and stepped in quietly, sneaking around the corner to her room where she stowed the box with her dress beneath her bed. Quietly, she snuck back out to the living room at the sound of voices. She peeked her head into the room, where her parents and a third party sat conversing about some serious matter.

"I just can't believe she would do something so dangerous," Mrs. Mayler wavered as she grabbed her husband's hand. Mr. Mayler pursed his lips and ran his finger along his chin. "Lydia's never lied to us before."

"She's never lied to me either," a familiar voice said. "I'm just as— just as worried. Trust me, I am. All I care about is Lydia's safety, and I truly fear that she is in danger."

Lydia covered her hand over her mouth to muffle a gasp as she witnessed Cedric betray her.

"Thank you for bringing this to our attention, Cedric. You are such a good friend to Lydia. And to us. We don't know what we would do without you."

Cedric nodded and shook Mr. Mayler's hand. Lydia managed to hide from sight as he said his goodbyes. The Maylers still maintained their worried persona, but Lydia could tell by the look in their eyes they were deeply disappointed and angry. She waited until they were in the kitchen and couldn't see her, then opened and closed the front door to walk in as if nothing had happened. Taking a deep breath, she made her way into the kitchen and greeted her parents normally. They did not respond in the same manner.

"It's a little late, isn't it?" Mrs. Mayler asked, but it wasn't really a question.

Lydia shrugged. "I lost track of time, I suppose."

"Doing what?"

Lydia froze. She couldn't use Cedric as an excuse anymore, and every past excuse was now useless. "I was. . .on a walk. And I got lost. In the woods."

They didn't look convinced, but Lydia pretended as if she had persuaded them. She poured herself a glass of water and hid the perspiration on her forehead.

Mrs. Mayler sighed and folded her hands. "Lydia, I think we need to have an honest conversation here."

"About what?" *Yes, play dumb,* she thought. *That might work.*

"I think you know what."

Lydia shook her head and half-laughed to give herself a calm perception as she did her best to look confused. "No, I'm afraid I don't."

Mrs. Mayler's face suddenly became very red and she stood to her feet with an anger Lydia had never seen before. "Lydia Mayler, is it true that you have been sneaking away to that strange shop owned by Mr. Miller?"

Lydia's heart beat a little faster and her legs turned to jelly. She couldn't lie and pass it off as truth anymore. They knew. Even if she did lie convincingly, Cedric ruined every ounce of trust her parents held in her.

Lydia took a deep breath and muttered, "Yes."

Mr. Mayler turned away and ran his hands through his hair. His wife only grew angrier.

"You *know* what we've told you, Lydia. We've *told* you to stay away from that *place*. Why on earth would you think it was a good idea to go there?"

Lydia started to say something, but her mother cut her off.

"And with all of those—those—*freaks*! Those *freaks* that work there! No one in town even knows who Mr. Miller *is*!"

"Don't you *dare* call them freaks! They are *good* people!"

"Why, Lydia, why on *earth* could you possibly believe that this was a good thing to do? Your father and I have been worried *sick* about you, and you've just been *gallivanting* around without a single care. I don't even—I don't think I can even *believe*—did you *drink* anything?"

"What? No! What is wrong with you?" Lydia exclaimed. "Cedric really let you have it, didn't he?"

"Leave Cedric out of this. It isn't the poor boy's fault what you've done."

That did it for Lydia. "Of course. *Nothing* is *ever* Cedric's fault. It's always *my* fault, isn't it? Well, if wanting to be free is a fault, then consider me guilty! But I refuse to apologize for something that has only brought me a greater joy than anything else in this—this *boring* life has!"

As soon as the words left Lydia's mouth, she knew she made a mistake. Her mother scoffed, but no words left her mouth. Lydia breathed heavily in anticipation.

"You—are *never* to go there again." Mrs. Mayler sided next to her husband, who had remained silent the whole argument.

"What? Mother, you can't! Father, please. . ." Lydia tried to bring him to her side, but he shook his head.

"If you *ever* even *think* about going down Dandelion Lane again, I will never let you leave this house again. Do you understand?"

Lydia's eyes burned as she formulated a plan in the back of her mind. "*Fine*! I really hope you're happy!" She turned and ran to her room and slammed the door. Her mother screamed back, "And don't even *think* about leaving your room for the next week!"

Lydia fumed, pacing back and forth in thought. If she couldn't leave, how could she make it back to find Zabuli? She *had* to leave. But when? And *how*?

Then, it dawned on her.

When her parents fell asleep, she would sneak out. She would have to make sure to be quiet and careful enough with the door, but she could do it.

Now it was only a matter of waiting. Though exhausted, Lydia forced herself to remain alert and awake until the moon was in the middle of the sky. She began to leave, but a faint guilt tugged at her heart and convicted her to at least leave a letter on her bed:

To Mother and Father,

I cannot continue to live a life in which I have no interest. I love you both so much, but this isn't about you. It's about me. If I don't come back home, please don't come looking for me. Give the shop to Henry when he's ready, and know that I am content with my choices. Thank you for all you have done for me, but it's time I grow up and make my own decisions.

Don't come after me. Please.

—Lydia

She folded the letter and placed it on her pillow. With a final sigh, she nodded to herself and crept out from her doorway, careful of the creaking wood below her feet. Slowly, she made her way past her parent's room and around the corner. At the bottom edge of the hallway, she turned past the kitchen, then past the sitting room, until she could see the door. Lydia smiled to herself and approached quickly, until a loud bark separated her from her socks.

"Rosie, stop!" Lydia whispered frantically, trying to silence the yapping dog. Rosie disregarded Lydia's pleas and continued barking. Upstairs, Lydia heard a rustling and a few quiet murmurs. "I'm going to miss you, clueless thing."

She flung the door open, closed it carefully, then fled into the night with the echo of barking still in her ears.

Lydia hadn't the slightest clue where she would go. In any other instance, she would flee to Cedric's, but that would only condemn her further. All of the shops were locked and closed. She couldn't stay out in the dark.

So, with the solution that always seemed to be the best, Lydia found herself outside of Mr. Miller's shop in the cold darkness of night. She tried the door handle, which luckily opened with a slight jiggle.

Lydia had never seen the shop so dark. It was completely pitch black, with only a few streams of moonlight illuminating the pathways and shelves. Quietly, she looked around to see if Bastien was present, but she didn't hear or see anything. With a breath of relief, she relaxed into the chair behind the counter and rubbed her tired eyes.

But, at once, she was awakened by the valiant cry of a silhouette leaping from the shadows. She screamed, then swung her hand back and slapped as hard as she could. The cry was cut off with a thump to the floor, then followed by a pouting scoff.

"Bastien! What is *wrong* with you?" Lydia exclaimed.

"Me? *You're* the one who almost took my head off!" He rubbed his cheek and stuck out his bottom lip. "I thought you were an intruder."

"How could you possibly have an intruder when you and Mr. Miller don't let anyone in the shop?"

Bastien raised his finger, as if presenting a point, then crossed his arms. "Well, terror often causes a short bit of memory loss. What are you doing here in the middle of the night? We weren't expecting you for a few more hours."

Lydia plopped back into the chair and put her head in her hands, making lazy circles with her feet. "It was either now, or never leave my room again."

Bastien sighed. "Was it Cedric?"

Lydia nodded.

"I'm so sorry, dear. That must've been hard."

"It was. Is."

Then Lydia let it be silent for a while. It was pleasant. Calm. It appeared that she never had the opportunity to be still and think. She enjoyed the moment while it lasted, for in the quiet light she could feel herself drifting off to sleep. The last thing she remembered was a warm coat being draped over her as she dozed off in that dusty old chair she loved so dearly.

* * *

Lydia woke to warm sunbeams cascading down her cheeks. Bastien's jacket was draped over her. For a moment, she remained confused as to where she was. When the memories hit her, she wished they hadn't.

"Good morning again, Lydia." Bastien gave her a small muffin with blueberries and a pink wrapper. "I hope you're good and awake."

She rubbed her eyes and stretched her arms above her head. "I am now."

"Doesn't look like it."

Taking the muffin, she gave Bastien a half-hearted smile. "Thank you."

Mr. Miller was still fixing his shirt and hair when he cheerily passed by the counter. "Oh, hello, Lydia. You're back early."

"I didn't have much of a choice."

He gave her a sympathetic look, but said nothing more on the matter (which Lydia was grateful for). He glanced into a dusty mirror and fixed his hair. Once he was happy with the way it looked, he pulled two little sacks from his coat and handed one to both her and Bastien.

"In the case you might need them," Mr. Miller told them. "Good when you're in a pinch."

"What's in it?" Bastien asked.

"Exactly what you'll need."

Lydia furrowed her brow, but kept the pouch with her nonetheless. Just in case the worse ensued.

Mr. Miller arranged for Pippin to stay in the shop for the time being (as to not frighten any of the people in the crowd they encountered in Brightmeadow). He explained to him that even though the shop would *technically* be with us because he had the charm with him, Pippin would be able to leave out the front (in the case of an emergency), but he wouldn't be able to get back in. Lydia could tell Pippin was the slightest bit upset he wasn't included in their adventure, yet Lydia noticed the relief in his eyes. After Pippin left to go tidy up the back of the shop (busy work assigned by Mr. Miller), Mr. Miller pulled Lydia aside from the others and took the necklace from around his neck.

"Lydia. I need you to keep this for me."

Taken aback, she replied, "Are you serious?"

"Perfectly."

"Mr. Miller, I can't do that. I can't keep your shop for you, that's *way* too serious. What if Zabuli gets you?"

"She doesn't have me if she doesn't have the shop. This charm here contains everything important about me that she desires. It will be much safer in the hands of another." He held it out to her. "Now, please. Just take it and keep it safe."

After thinking it over and seeing the desperate look in his eyes, Lydia took the necklace from him and draped it around her neck. She hid it under the top of her dress and prayed it would be safe there.

"Alright. Bastien, Lydia. We have to go through the marketplace get to Dahlia Road. Lydia, once we get there, we'll need you to do the talking to Zabuli, or, I suppose, Mrs. Fisher."

"What if she . . . I don't know about this, Mr. Miller," Lydia said. He took her hand and squeezed it tightly. "I promise we won't let anything happen to you. Bastien and I will be right here. And no matter what happens, it is imperative that she doesn't find out I am looking for her until the very last moment. Got it?"

Lydia gulped and nodded.

"Just be careful. Witches can be tricky. They mess with your mind and your senses."

So, after covering themselves with cloaks (which, in Lydia's opinion, made them stand out even more), the three snuck out down Magnolia Lane towards Dahlia Road.

Lydia recalled the last time she had walked this trail to Mrs. Fisher's house: her and Cedric talking, laughing, occasionally throwing flowers off Mrs. Fisher's bouquets.

So much had changed.

The smell of salt tingled Lydia's nose as they approached the start of Dahlia, the waves of the sea curling along the white sand beside the beautiful houses. Lydia removed the hood from her cloak and led the others towards the front of Mrs. Fisher's house.

"My. . ." Bastien marveled. "This really *is* a castle."

"Just stay hidden," Lydia said. "I'll try to be quick."

Bastien and Mr. Miller hid around the corner of the house, careful not to cause too much of a ruckus arguing over who could peek around the corner. Lydia, her heart beating through her chest and her knuckles white, knocked once, twice, then three times on the door.

A moment later, a handsome gentleman with a funny mustache opened the door.

"May I help you?"

Lydia gulped and faked a smile. "Yes, hello, I'm here to speak to Za—Mrs. Fisher? I'm Mrs. Mayler's daughter from the flower shop. My mother was wondering if Mrs. Fisher needed to place an order for her upcoming ball, since we haven't heard from her yet."

"I'm sorry, Mrs. Mayler, but Mrs. Fisher is currently unavailable."

Lydia's heart sank. "Unavailable? Do you mind if I ask why?"

"She's off on a walk, of course. She's out picking wild strawberries in the woods to make jam tonight."

Oh, no, Lydia thought, *the woods!* She knew what they were up to, and she was already a step ahead.

"If you'd like, you may come in and stay for tea until she returns," the man offered.

"Oh, no, no thank you, sir." Lydia started down the road. "I really must be going."

The second the door closed, Mr. Miller and Bastien followed after her. She filled them in on what the butler had said.

"Oh, dear," Mr. Miller murmured. "This isn't ideal."

"What do we do now?" Bastien leaned against a tree with a defeated look.

Mr. Miller grabbed his shoulders and steadied him. "*Not* give up, that's for sure. We'll have to go find her ourselves. She already knows we're after her, so we haven't got much of a choice."

"Are you sure that's a good idea?" Lydia asked.

"No, but we have to do something. Come on, now, we haven't any time to waste."

With quick feet and shaky breaths, the three started into the dense forest.

Lydia didn't remember the trees being so tall and the grass so thick. At last, she built the courage up to step off the trail and go deeper into the leaves and sticks branching for miles and miles in every direction.

"Those cloaks are a lot hotter than they look," Bastien complained. "I'm sweating up a storm over here."

"How can you sweat if you're a mannequin?" Lydia asked.

Bastien scoffed. "If I *weren't* a mannequin, maybe I *would* be sweaty."

The farther they traveled, the more Lydia started to lose focus. She could've sworn she had seen that tree over there a few times, but she didn't remember the small creek on her left. Mr. Miller encouraged them multiple times, but she was beginning to worry they were really lost.

"Don't be frightened," Mr. Miller said. "Evil feeds off fear."

"Well, *that's* not frightening at all," Lydia remarked. "Listen, I don't know where we are. I've never been this deep in the woods and I fear that we won't be able to get back out."

"Lydia, that's the *point*. We're looking for a witch, here. She's not going to be in the middle of town."

"How will we even know when we find the witch? Actual people live in these woods too, you know. *Normal* people. What are we going to do? Just barge in on an old man drinking tea and demand that he turn a mannequin into a human?"

"I'm human first, *then* mannequin."

Lydia rolled her eyes. "You know what I mean. Mrs. Fisher could be anywhere in these woods. How on earth are we going to find her?"

"Just by doubting yourself, it shows that she is already at work." Mr. Miller looked suspiciously. "Wherever she is, she's onto us."

Mr. Miller hurried ahead with a pace quicker than they had been accustomed to. Lydia and Bastien could hardly keep up due to the branches and leaves pulling at their sleeves. Bastien managed to hang onto the edge of Mr. Miller's cloak and keep up with his twists and turns. Lydia stayed close for a while, but she swore she heard a rustling noise behind her that sounded too loud for a forest creature. She jumped around in search of the disturbance, but there was nothing in sight. Sighing, she moved to follow the trail of Mr. Miller. When she looked back his way, he was nowhere in sight.

Lydia's arms turned to jelly. Alone, in the woods, with a witch that's out to get them all. The perfect combination! She groaned and started forward, but it was clear there were no footprints to be found.

"Of course. The *one* time we make Pippin stay home," she grumbled to herself as she sauntered through the dead leaves and moss. Eventually, the only hope she had left was to call for her friends. She knew she would happen upon *someone's* house in time, but for now, calling was all she could do.

"Mr. Miller! Bastien!" she called, as if she were beckoning a dog. She continued this on for a few more minutes, then gave up hope. Even if they *did* somehow hear her, it would confuse them trying to find their way back to a distant voice in the woods.

So, Lydia continued her hunt in the forest with a begrudging attitude. At least the shadows of the trees blocked the sun from her eyes and kept her cool, she thought. But that was all the good thinking she could do at the moment. Just when she was ready to take a breather and sit under a shady oak tree, she noticed a sweet smell in the air: the smell of lavender and honey, something of which was usually not present in the natural woods. She followed where her nose led her.

In the thick of the trees, a stone pathway led up to a small clearing with a nice, little cottage in the middle. Though it was in the middle of the woods, it was well kept, with flowers and ivy growing alongside the white walls. Smoke puffed out from the chimney and birds flew in and out of pink birdhouses decorated on the front lawn. Lydia hadn't ever seen this place before, and the fact that she was going in alone did *not* make her feel any better. She was very much aware of the possibility that a witch could live here, but it looked all too fluffy and appealing for any evil entity to have a hold of it. Besides, if it *really* were a witch in the house, why would it not be more secretive? It was probably just one of the older townspeople. Quite a few of them lived out in these woods. Still, even with the reassurance, she couldn't shake the feeling of suspicion that flickered through her mind. Mr. Miller and Bastien were no doubt nearby and she knew she was safe, but something unnerved her—something she couldn't quite put her finger on. *Perhaps it's the fear of being alone*, she thought. *What more could it be?*

With a deep breath, she knocked on the door and waited. A few moments later, a pretty young lady answered the door with a chipper smile, and an all too familiar voice.

"Lydia Mayler? What are you doing here?"

"Oh, I was just out for a walk and—well—if I'm honest I'm not really sure where I'm going, and I was hoping to ask for some help." Lydia forced a smile. "I hope that's alright."

"Of course it is. May I ask how you're doing?"

"I'm quite well, Ms. Candy. I hope the same for you."

Ms. Candy smiled, and by the tone of her voice, Lydia could tell she didn't have visitors often. Lydia had always assumed she would live someplace like Dahlia Road, where she could flaunt her men and nice clothes like all the other pretty ladies with money did. Her voice sounded inviting—an invitation Lydia trusted, yet remained weary of. Lydia had never *liked* Ms. Candy, of course, but she was no threat. Unless, of course, you were a young woman looking for a husband in Brightmeadow. Besides, Lydia didn't have a list of other options at the moment.

"Come in, dear. The mosquitoes are horrible at this time of day."

Lydia glanced behind her shoulder, then stepped inside the cozy cottage. Everything about it was just as Lydia expected: the smell of fresh bread and strawberries, assortments of trinkets inside in little glass shelves, and figurines arranged in strangely human positions. The decor was all very cute, but the amount of trinkets gave the whole cottage a sort of uncomfortable feeling. Lydia chalked it up to just be the unfamiliarity. New places always made her feel anxious, especially when they were extremely cluttered. A ginger cat wandered about and rubbed her head against Lydia's leg. She stooped down to scratch its head.

"Penny loves visitors," Ms. Candy giggled. "Have a seat. I'll make you some tea."

Lydia took a seat at a white wooden table and watched Ms. Candy bounce around the kitchen. Lydia wondered how someone could be so bubbly when everyone in town ostracized and taunted her. So much, in fact, that Ms. Candy hardly knew *anyone* in town (besides the few suitors she reeled in). Rather secretive, but Lydia was beginning to understand why. Suddenly, she felt a terrible guilt settle over her. People were so unkind to Ms. Candy that she couldn't even make it to the edge of Magnolia Street without being ushered back to her house by off-hand comments and rude glares. Lydia felt partially responsible for this. Ms. Candy, after all, seemed to be a very kind person. So what if she was a bit of a tramp?

"How's your mother been? I know she's always so busy during this time of year." Ms. Candy asked politely.

Another pang of guilt, straight to the heart. "She's—she's alright."

Ms. Candy eyed Lydia knowingly with a touch of pity. "I know that tone all too well. Troubles with your mother?"

Lydia nodded.

"Don't be so down about it. Everyone gets into disagreements. Even over small things." Ms. Candy sprinkled in an assortment of leaves and tea into a kettle and placed it on a small flame.

Lydia half-chuckled to herself. "Well. . .*this* wasn't a small thing."

"Oh, dear. What happened?"

Lydia opened her mouth to say something, then closed it. "Actually, I don't—I don't really think I should talk about it."

Ms. Candy poured the tea into a flowered teacup and sat it in front of Lydia. "No worries, dear. You can tell me anything. I'm a very private person, you see."

A private person? Perhaps that's why Ms. Candy was so ostracized, Lydia thought. People in Brightmeadow are very social, and if you aren't willing to be out-going, friends were hard to come by. Come to think of it, Lydia couldn't remember seeing Ms. Candy out and about that often (every time she found a new man, of course, but other than that, nothing). Lydia brushed away the strange thought and attributed it to personal privacy. If Lydia were her, *she* wouldn't want people poking their noses in her business, either.

"It's all a very complicated matter," Lydia said.

"Drink some tea," Ms. Candy encouraged. "It'll make you feel better."

Lydia took a sip. It was sweet and tasted like lavender and sage with a hint of honey.

"Wonderful tea," Lydia commented, sipping it once more, then again, then again.

Ms. Candy smiled, then rested her head in her hand and watched Lydia with a sympathetic gaze. "Tell me your troubles, dear. Soon they'll feel so far away."

Suddenly, Lydia felt much too full of words. All the emotions hit her at once, and it was everything she could do to not speak upon the matter.

"So much is changing, you know? I mean, I just lost my only friend because I didn't want to get married and he did, and *then* he went and told my parents I've been sneaking off, which is really only half true—well, I guess it's fully true. And now, I'm going to lose *all* of my friends. Now Cedric won't ever talk to me again, and I suppose I won't ever talk to him, either."

"Sneaking off?" Ms. Candy tilted her head. "Where on earth can you sneak off to in Brightmeadow?"

"I know, right?" Lydia shook her head a little too dramatically and sipped her tea again. "It's so incredibly boring here! Which is why when I found that strange old shop on the edge of Dandelion Lane, I *had* to know what was in there."

Suddenly, her interest was piqued. She leaned in closer with an odd sort of smile. "What kind of strange shop?"

"Well, I went in one day and met this mannequin who came to life! And then, there was a talking toad! Who could sing!"

"A talking, singing toad?" Ms. Candy marveled.

"Yes! I was just as surprised as you!" Lydia finished the last sip of tea. "So, when Mr. Miller brought me to all of those magnificent places, you can't blame me for wanting to go with him, can you?" Lydia didn't even know what she was saying anymore. The words just kept spilling out and she wasn't able to stop them. "I've seen the most amazing things. This place called Carmen, and then I went dancing, and then I went into paintings, and Mr. Miller is apparently a wizard, but he also said he's not a very good wizard, so I'm not quite sure what to think about that."

Ms. Candy smiled widely. Lydia knew she was smiling because she was pleased with her company, but there was a weird look behind her smile that made Lydia the slightest bit uncomfortable.

"Oh, I know. Vincent really is the lousiest wizard there is."

Lydia hardly heard her. "Tell me about it. He won't even cast spells to do basic *chores*. I mean, if you can do magic, then why not take advantage of it? If *I* were a wizard I'd—"

Lydia stopped. Something was wrong. Something was off. She could feel it. But what was it? A fatigue fell over her, along with a dizzy head. She tried to shake it away, but it only made it worse. She glanced behind her and suddenly noticed a whole array of mannequins she swore weren't there before. Lydia blinked, then looked around to try and focus on something else to make her eyes go back to normal.

"Something the matter dear?"

Lydia shook her head wearily. "No, no it's just—" She looked towards the corner of the kitchen, where a vial of glimmering dust shimmered in a jar. "What—what is that?"

Ms. Candy looked back, then half-chuckled. "Oh, don't worry about that. Just a tad bit of golden dust."

"Golden dust?" Lydia furrowed her brow.

Ms. Candy rolled her eyes playfully. "Of course. How else would I be able to do my magic?" She stood fixed her dress, then went over and added a pinch of the golden dust into a large, wooden bowl.

"Do. . .magic? But I thought. . .only witches can do magic."

"Oh, don't talk too much, dear, you might hurt yourself." She stirred the mixture, which puffed out pink rings of smoke. "You've already told me what I needed to know. So just hush and take a deep breath."

Lydia squinted and tried to stand, but it was no use. She was much too dizzy, much too tired. Ms. Candy came over to her and knelt to her level, then reached around her neck and pulled the charm necklace off her neck. Lydia opened her mouth to protest. Ms. Candy shushed her with a single finger to her lips.

"That's mine," Lydia blurted. "Why did you—why would you want that?"

"Shh, Lydia. Vincent doesn't need to know."

Vincent? Lydia thought, *Who is Vin—*

Oh, no.

"How do you know Mr. Miller?" Lydia demanded through droopy eyes.

Ms. Candy giggled. "I might have sold him a spell or two. A rather handsome man, isn't he? And that lovely friend of his, Bastien. . .such a shame he didn't understand true beauty. Did he?"

"You know Bastien?"

She scoffed and flipped her hair over her shoulder to look at Lydia. "Darling, you really don't understand, do you?"

Lydia ran through the incoherent thoughts in her head. They were all mushed together, but in the end all she could remember was the last five minutes. A few names popped up here and there, but the fatigue weighed on her more every second.

"What was in that tea?" Lydia murmured, picking up the cup and examining it. When she turned it over, a few specks of glimmering dust fell out. Lydia's heart fell. "You're. . .you're a witch," she realized. Ms. Candy hummed in response and nodded. Lydia's heart began to beat a little faster. "And. . .you know Bastien and Mr. Miller, and you said you—"

Ms. Candy leaned towards her expectantly. And, though she didn't want to believe it, Lydia understood.

"You're Zabuli," she uttered. "Aren't you?"

Ms. Candy curtsied and stirred the bowl. "Wonderful, dear. I really was worried you weren't going to get that."

"Wait—but that means—"

"It means a lot of things, darling, no need to go through them all."

"But you can make Bastien human again. And Antoinette." Lydia perked up the last bit of hope she had. "You can break the spell."

Ms. Candy crouched to her level, sticking her lip out with a mocking pity. "You can't break spells, dear. Everyone knows that. Except for lousy wizards, I suppose."

That's when the real fear kicked in. Even though Lydia's adrenaline worked in overdrive, she couldn't bring herself to stand or hardly even move under the heavy fatigue blanketing her.

Mrs. Candy clapped her hands. "All finished! Perfect." She poured the mix into a glass vial and corked the top of it. "Thank you, Lydia dear. At last, I have found that sneaky Vincent Miller. He's slipped through my fingers one too many times. How lucky a naive little girl would just so happen upon my woodsy cottage and spill the beans." She smirked. "How pleased he will be to hear of such things."

"What are you going to do?" Lydia's voice wavered.

Ms. Candy waved her hand in the air. "Oh, that's none of your concern. All I want is his past. It won't be too difficult to get. Thanks to you." She smirked and ran her fingers along the edge of a wilted flower on the countertop.

"You won't get away with this," Lydia sneered. "That charm isn't yours to toy with."

Ms. Candy laughed. "Oh, silly, it isn't the charm I want." She grabbed a handful of dark powder from the jar and played with it in her hand. "It's Vincent."

With an evil chuckle, the woman threw the dust in the air. In a split second, Lydia was falling. Ms. Candy disappeared with the shop charm and potion as well as the information Lydia had spilled, and all Lydia could do was fall.

And fall.

And fall.

The light dimmed from above her as she tried to fight against the magic, but when she finally hit the ground, the world went dark.

13

When Lydia opened her eyes and lifted her head, she could hardly see anything through the dull light. High above her was an escape, but down in this cavern, it was impossible to make it up to the top. The sound of dripping water echoed around her on the dark rocks and wet walls. Lydia stood and tried to climb the edges of the rocks, but couldn't make it farther than a foot. She tried, then tried again, but all she did was cut her hands on the brittle edges of the cavern walls.

The memory of Ms. Candy came back to her. Lydia's breathing grew heavy when she realized what she had done. Her only friends, and it was *her* fault they were in danger. How stupid she was! Why did she drink that tea? Why did she do that? Her friends were in danger because of her, and all she could do was sit at the bottom of a deep cavern full of guilt.

She tried to climb, but it was no use. She tried to jump and catch a break in the rocks, but that didn't work, either. She was running out of options. She squinted at the top of the cavern and, in a desperate attempt, tried to call for help.

"Mr. Miller!" She called. "Mr. Miller! Bastien!"

Only the sound of dripping water replied. Lydia grew more desperate with each passing second.

"Bastien!" She screamed. "Bastien, I'm stuck! I'm stuck down here! Pippin! Pippin, can you hear me? Can anybody hear me?"

Her voice echoed up to the top of the cavern hole, but no voice echoed back down to her. Lydia's eyes stung and suddenly her chest felt very heavy.

"Hugo!" She screamed with all of her last strength. "Hugo! Hugo, please! Please. . ."

Defeated, she slumped down against the wall and hugged her knees to her chest. When she finally gave in, the tears fell down her bruised cheeks and shaking hands. She held herself tighter, doing her best to stay calm, but she didn't *want* to be calm`. Lydia had never known true fear, but it was in this very moment she understood.

She tried to call again, but all that escaped her voice was a raspy cry.

"*Hugo.*"

Time passed by, no more than a half hour. Lydia shivered in fear and in the cold air. The water had soaked her hair and her dress sending shivers down her arms. Soon her eyes grew heavy. Just as she began to drift off to sleep, a small voice snapped her back to life.

"Hello?" It was a quiet call from a creature with a sweet, familiar voice.

Lydia jumped to her feet at once and reached as far as she could up to the top of the cavern. "Hello! Help, I'm stuck! My name is Lydia Mayler, please help me!"

"Lydia?" The voice exclaimed. A face peaked into the cavern.

"Pippin! Oh, Pippin, I'm so glad to see you!"

"Wait there, m'lady! I'm on my way down!" Pippin strapped his harp onto his back, then carefully climbed his way down the cavern, using his toad legs and arms to navigate down the bumpy rocks. At last, he reached the bottom, and Lydia grabbed him tightly.

"How did you find me?"

Pippin wiped away a tear on her face. "I don't know. I suppose I just followed my heart. And the wind. The wind is very important." Her sorrows were forgotten for just a moment. "I've always been rather good at finding people exactly when they needed to be found. Maybe that's my magic."

Lydia smiled at his sweet innocence, then looked to the top of the cavern. "I suppose we're both stuck now. Aren't we?" She slumped against the wall and stared up at the faint light streaming in.

"At least we aren't alone," Pippin reassured, but Lydia didn't feel any better. Suddenly, she could not contain her sadness anymore. "Oh, Pippin, this is all my fault." She put her head in her hands as Pippin watched her sadly. He comforted her with a nice hug on the side of her arm, but Lydia felt no better. "I'm so sorry I drug you into all of this."

"M'lady Lydia, to die for my love would be my highest honor." He meant well, but it only made Lydia feel worse.

"I don't know what I'm to do," she cried. "Mr. Miller is stuck with Bastien, all of my friends are in danger, and I don't know how to help. I should've never set foot in that old shop! I just ruined the lives of all the people in this world I care about."

Pippin sighed and slumped next to her. He strummed his harp mindlessly in thought as Lydia listened. It sounded familiar.

"Can you play me something, Pippin?" she asked. "Please?"

His harp strummed. "Alright. How about something familiar?" He continued, "Oh and once my eyes did see, the spell a witch once put on me,

To love her til' the end of time, the face of beauty most sublime,

Until she rests her precious head, no sooner will my love be dead,

Golden dust was once the key, for peace throughout eternity,

Now see my sorrows once were bare—"

"Wait a moment!" Lydia exclaimed, interrupting Pippin's song. "Sing that part again!"

"Which part?"

"The part about—the last—the last few lines you did! Sing them again."

Though confused, he complied. "Oh and once my eyes did see, the spell a witch once put on me,

To love her til' the end of time, the face of beauty most sublime,

Until she rests her precious head, no sooner will my love be dead—"

"That's it!" Lydia jumped up so quickly she knocked the poor bard and his harp over. Apologizing, she helped him to his feet and paced frantically back and forth. "Mr. Miller once said that the only person who could break a spell was the one who cast it. According to Zabuli, that was false, but what if it really isn't?"

Pippin tilted his head to the side. "I don't understand."

"What if the person who cast the spell couldn't *directly* undo it, but had to have something done to them?" Pippin still looked confused. "What if when the witch dies, the spell dies with her?"

His eyes perked up. "'Until she rests her precious head, no sooner will my love be dead!' Lydia! That's it!"

"We need to get to Mr. Miller *now*," she exclaimed, gathering herself up and pacing around the small space. "But how?"

"What would Mr. Miller do?" Pippin said.

"Who knows? He thinks unlike anyone I've ever met." She pulled out the small pouch he gave her from her pocket and sifted through it. "I mean, look at all this! A piece of paper, two copper coins, a stone dragonfly, an empty vial, a—wait!" Lydia pulled out the dragonfly and held it above her head. "The dragonfly! If I move the wing like so—" Lydia moved the wing to the side and in an instant, the bug expanded in size. Lifting up her skirt, she put herself on the front seat and flicked a few buttons on the side of the wheel. She really didn't know what she was doing, but *eventually* she would press the right thing. At the turn of a curly knob, the wings buzzed, and the plane started up. "Hop on, Pippin!"

Pippin gulped, then climbed up the side and onto the seat behind her. "Please be gentle."

Lydia took a deep breath and moved a lever that made them hover a few feet off the ground. Gripping the steering wheel tightly, she glanced back at Pippin. "Ready?"

"I don't think—" But before he could finish, Lydia had slammed her foot into the pedal pulled the wheel towards her, sending the dragonfly speeding towards the narrow exit. "Are we going to make it?" Pippin screamed.

Bracing herself, Lydia put more pressure onto the pedal until it was digging into the floor. "I think so!"

"Do you know how to fly this thing?" Pippin held on for dear life in the back.

"Not really!"

With a single burst of speed, the dragonfly sailed out of the cavern and into the blue sky above. Lydia didn't recognize the ground below her anymore, but she was just relieved they made it out. Pippin shook in the backseat with his eyes covered.

"Pippin! We made it!" Lydia exclaimed, clapping her hands. Pippin peeked through his fingers at the height, then screamed and covered his eyes again. Lydia laughed, then tapped the compass on the wheel. Honestly, she didn't know why she did that. It wouldn't help. She had no idea where she was going in the first place.

"Pippin! How did you say that you found me again?"

Pippin gulped. "I said I followed my heart. And the wind. I don't know how, really, it just happened!"

"If you found me, that means you can find Mr. Miller. Now, focus!" Lydia moved the steering wheel to the left. "Which way should I go?"

"I don't know if I can, Lydia. I only have so much magic in me to use."

"We need to try," Lydia insisted. "*Please.*"

He shifted nervously, then sighed. "Alright. I'll try my hardest." He took a deep breath and closed his eyes, as if he were speaking to Mr. Miller in his mind. Lydia kept glancing back at him, then back at the sky ahead of her. Suddenly, Pippin perked up.

"Hard left!"

Lydia yanked the wheel to the left and sent them flying down. Pippin shrieked.

"What now?"

Pippin squeezed his eyes shut. "Go straight. And hurry!"

Lydia pushed the pedal again, sending the dragonfly zooming and earning another cry from Pippin. She steadied the wheel.

The longer they continued forward, the darker the sky became. Lydia wasn't sure if she was still in Brightmeadow, or in some random place Zabuli banished her to. But, by the looks of the grey clouds, Lydia feared she was far from Brightmeadow.

"Go right, but only just a little bit," Pippin said. "We're almost there, I can feel it."

"I think I feel it, too."

They entered into a thick cloud that blinded their sight. Lydia hung onto the wheel tightly. The clouds broke and revealed a dark forest with a tall castle twirling above the trees. Lydia wouldn't describe it as evil-looking, but when she gazed at the white stone and silver on the twirling marble, an uneasy feeling overcame her—a feeling of which Lydia could not explain.

Lydia brought the dragonfly down into the tree branches for better cover. After circling around for a few minutes and flicking levers and buttons, she managed to land it just well enough to keep her and Pippin from flying off into the trees. The dragonfly buzzed to the forest ground and landed amongst the leaves. Lydia jumped off the second it hit the ground. Pippin, still shaken, slowly climbed off and laid in the grass to regain his bearings. Lydia flicked the wings back into the sides of the plane and shrunk it down. She placed it back in her pouch and coerced Pippin out of his fit of terror.

"Pippin, you were fantastic. Thank you." Lydia hugged him and stood him back on his feet. He gulped, then followed Lydia closely as she snuck her way up to the edge of the castle. After examining the walls, Lydia found a door jammed shut just hiding behind a stack of wood. After kicking and jabbing at it with rocks, she managed to bust the lock open. Her and Pippin crept up a stone staircase lit with torches. Pippin croaked.

"Lydia, are you sure this is a good idea?"

"Come on." She nodded her head for Pippin to follow her to the next room down a wide hallway. Halfway down, she noticed a door on the left side. Creaking it open, it led them down another stone staircase.

When they reached the bottom, a sudden shiver ran down Lydia's spine. It was cold and uninviting. Either side of the room was lined with cells, all of which were empty except for one on the far corner. Glancing nervously at Pippin, Lydia snuck down the side of the wall and peeked behind the bars. Her heart sank.

"Bastien!" She cried, reaching her hands through the metal. "Are you alright?"

Bastien gripped her hands with a sigh of relief. "Oh, Lydia! Thank the heavens you're here! I'm even happy to see *you*, Pippin."

Disregarding his comment, Lydia asked, "Where's Mr. Miller?"

"Zabuli's got him! She's trying to steal his past!"

"His past? What does that mean?"

Bastien hesitated. "I can't tell you."

"What? Bastien you can't be serious."

"I promised Hugo I would never tell a soul."

Lydia sighed, then squeezed Bastien's hands. "I understand, Bastien. But listen to me." She squeezed his hand a bit tighter. "If you don't tell me what's going on, Mr. Miller will *die*, and you will never see him again, and you'll be cursed to this form for the rest of your days. *Bastien*. You *have* to trust me."

He hung his head down and sighed. "If you must know. . .I'll tell you." He thought for a moment. "When we were all in our younger years, Hugo and Zabuli happened to meet in the gardens of Goya when their school brought them there for a lesson on magic. Zabuli pursued him, but Hugo never gave in. Laurie never had a good feeling about her. After—"

"Wait," Lydia interrupted, "*Who* is Laurie?"

Bastien bit the inside of his lip. He reached into his shirt and revealed a golden locket in the shape of a book. He motioned for Lydia to open it. She did.

Inside, there was a small, black and white photograph of three people. She assumed the two men in it were Bastien and Mr. Miller. The third was a woman whom Lydia did not recognize, but she seemed to bear quite the resemblance to Lydia.

"That's Laurie." He pointed to the lady. "Hugo's sister."

Lydia stopped breathing. "His *sister?*"

He nodded. "Yes, his little sister. She went on many an adventure with us. Her and Zabuli never really got along. Laurie always was quite protective of Hugo. And for good reason." He swallowed hard. "Zabuli wanted the adventures as well, but we soon found out for wrong reasons."

"Wrong reasons?"

"Hugo's been to countless places and been around countless magicians of importance. If Zabuli was along with him, she could've gained access to all of the golden dust and magic realms if she wanted to. The three of us though. . .we never let her get too close to us."

"Then what happened?"

Bastien put the locket back inside of his shirt. "Laurie. . .she was like no one else. Brave, exciting, and so full of life. One day she went out on a journey to the lands of Toska after she heard of some unrest in the city. Magic control, you see. A new group of dark magicians had infiltrated the city with plans to clean it all out. Hugo didn't get there until it was too late." He brought his gaze down. "She died. To save a child from the blade of a sword." Lydia's eyes welled with tears. She could only imagine the pain and anguish Mr. Miller had been through. Losing his sister. . . "He had to watch her die. And there was nothing he could do about it. When he came to find me, Zabuli beat him. After I refused to tell her what Hugo was up to, she grew angry. She thought if she found a way to pull his past from me, she could steal Hugo with ease. After I refused to tell her anything, well. . ." He brought his eyes downcast. "I never got the chance to escape."

"Bastien, I'm so sorry," she consoled. "I had no idea."

"You weren't *supposed* to ever know." He gripped the bars tightly. "It's his darkest memory. He thought Brightmeadow might make it better. He was only ever fooling himself."

"But Zabuli. . .why does she want his past?"

"If Zabuli takes his past, she can rewrite his history for herself. Like I said, Hugo's been on dozens of adventures and saved even more people—people of grand importance. The fairies, the magicians of Goya, the sorcerers of Velho . . . If Zabuli can write herself in, she'll have access to *all* of it. The Hugo we know today will be completely gone. He will have never even *existed*. And Zabuli? She'll have full control over every magical realm in existence."

Lydia's breath caught in her throat. "Oh, no." Pippin hung onto the end of her dress worriedly. "Pippin, stay here with Bastien. I'm going to find Mr. Miller." She started back down the hallway.

Pippin called after her, "Wait! You can't just leave us here alone!"

"I don't have any other choice! I promise I'll come back!" And with that, she sprinted up the stairs and into the unknown of the grand castle.

14

The castle was like a raggedy quilt. Each room was completely different than the last: tons of libraries, cauldron rooms, rooms filled with butterflies and other insects on display in glass containers, and rooms Lydia dared not enter. This only made it more difficult for Lydia to find her way around. It seemed with each staircase she climbed she went lower and each room she traveled sent her farther away. It was a maze, and Zabuli knew exactly how to trick Lydia.

At last, she stumbled upon a row of marble stairs reaching up into one of the towers. She snuck quietly up to the cracked door at the top. Peering inside, she saw Zabuli pacing around the room, and Mr. Miller tied with his arms behind his back in a really uncomfortable looking chair. Why the chair stood out to Lydia, she didn't know. She brushed off her incoherent thoughts and focused back onto the scene unfolding in front of her.

"You don't recall that day in Goya, do you?"

Mr. Miller groaned, "Believe me. I wish I couldn't."

"I think it would be in your best interest to keep your mouth *shut*." She leaned in close with the threat of some spell in her hand. Mr. Miller didn't flinch, but he gave the vial a nervous look. "You're utterly useless, sometimes. You know that?"

"You flatter me."

"You're impossible."

"Good."

Lydia tried to lean in closer, but almost toppled over into the room. Right before she hit the door, she caught herself.

"You know, it's probably a good thing they're all finished for already," she said. "I'm sure you wouldn't have been able to save them, anyway. It's better this way, isn't it?"

His face grew very red at once as he fought against the ropes. "Leave them out of this."

"She looked just like you." Zabuli tapped her finger on a photograph sitting on a desk with a *tsk, tsk*. "Just what the world needed. A *second* Vincent Miller."

She must mean Laurie, Lydia thought.

"Don't push it, Z."

"Z! No one's called me that in years." She chuckled darkly to herself and sighed. "Poor dear Laurie. That's what *she* used to call me."

He shifted uncomfortably and tried to move away when Zabuli suddenly leaned in very close. Her eyes glazed over the ring on his finger. She tapped it mockingly. "I see you still keep a part of her with you. Isn't that sweet?" She shoved him back with a hard hand. "At least you'll have good company when you make it to the other side. A whole *family* waiting for you? At least you've *had* people to care about you, Vincent. Not all of us are so lucky." She said the last part sorrowfully, hiding a hidden sadness that she desperately tried to push away as she lashed out—

Wait a moment, Lydia's thoughts interjected, a *whole* family?

"You still have this silly old shop," Zabuli sniggered, holding up the charm. "Keeping all of their things safe. *Why*, Vincent?"

"Oh, my soul," Lydia muttered to herself. The shop really wasn't a shop after all! Everything in there was a part of something much grander than she thought. It was his past, every memory of the people whom he had loved. That's why nothing was for sale, and *that's* why he stayed in Brightmeadow! No one would bother him, and he could keep all of his family's possessions safely and quietly.

Her heart broke into a thousand pieces.

The thought of everything this man had suffered through: the loss of his sister, his mother and father, Bastien, and Antoinette. . .it was too much to grasp.

Lydia clamped a hand over her mouth.

He sneered. "I wouldn't expect a heartless soul like you to understand."

She smiled mockingly. "You're right. But, none of that really matters anymore, does it? I'm probably doing you a favor, you know." She moved over to the desk in the corner and raised a vial of pure white powder into the air to admire it. "The man you used to be, the life you used to live, will all be gone. It'll all just be a forgotten memory, never to have existed. Won't it be nice?"

He yanked his hands with a desperate grunt, but the ties didn't budge.

"Don't fight it, Vincent," she said. "Don't fight the pain. I can take it all away. *I* can fix *everything*. No more suffering, no more sadness. . .you just have to let go."

"No," he replied sternly. "You're wrong."

She tilted her head to the side. "Perhaps. But there's only one way to find out."

"If you want to kill me, that's fine," he panted, "But my past doesn't belong to you. Who I am isn't yours to take."

"If you want something, you take it." Zabuli uncorked the vial. "And who said I wasn't going to kill you eventually?" She sprinkled the powder into her hands tortuously slow. Mr. Miller braced himself for whatever was about to happen, but Lydia couldn't watch any longer. If she didn't do something, Mr. Miller would cease to exist forever.

"Don't you touch him!" She barged into the room with no plan at all, which she immediately realized was a really horrible idea.

"Lydia!" Mr. Miller smiled.

"*You*!" Zabuli growled. "I thought I already took care of you."

"Apparently not, as I am standing right here, alive as ever." Mr. Miller snickered when she said this, but Zabuli did not find it so funny.

"You brat! You have absolutely *no* idea what you're interfering with."

"I do, Ms. Candy," Lydia said, "And I'm here to say that what you're about to do won't satisfy you."

"And why on earth do you figure that?"

"What I'm *saying* is, changing the past won't make your future any better." Lydia stepped a bit closer. "No matter what happens, fate doesn't change. Like a crystal ball: it doesn't matter what you do to try and avoid the fate it gives you, destiny trumps all."

That was obviously not the right thing to say, as Zabuli's face grew very red, and she looked as if she might explode at any moment. "You think I care about *fate*, Miss Mayler? Well, here's the truth for you: *I* am fate. *I* will be the past, present, future, and eternity. It doesn't matter what *fate* means. *I* will control what it means."

While she droned on, Lydia glanced around the room filled with small vials of varying powders and spells. Some books were half open on desks, some torn or burned. Candles melted onto tables and a collection of butterflies hung on the far wall.

"You can take his past if you'd like, but it's not going to change anything." Lydia stepped closer. "You'll still be the miserable, rotten *creature* you are now."

"Lydia, don't push it," Mr. Miller warned.

"He's right, you know. There's only so much a stupid little girl can do."

"I am *not* stupid."

Zabuli laughed. "Really? Then how'd I get this?" She dangled Mr. Miller's necklace from her hand. "All for a drink of tea."

Lydia blushed furiously out of anger and embarrassment. As hard as he tried, Mr. Miller could not hide the look of confusion, shame, and understanding that crossed his features at once.

"Lydia," he said seriously, "Get out of here before you can't any longer."

"I'm afraid she's already lost that chance." Zabuli flicked her wrist, and the door behind Lydia slammed shut. She flinched, but stood her ground with an unwavering expression of bravery.

"Don't you want to know how I got here?" Lydia asked with a plan brewing.

Zabuli raised her eyebrow, but said nothing. She shrugged with an expression that said *well?*

"I got here because someone who truly loves me stood by my side. Was it dangerous? Yes. Are they risking their life for me? Yes. But in the end, when someone truly loves you, you're willing to do that kind of thing. And you see, Ms. Candy, nothing you could've done would have changed that. I mean, you put a spell on me, banished me, and kidnapped two of my dearest friends, yet somehow I still found my way to be standing here right now." Lydia didn't really understand why she was trying to reason with an angry witch who had her mind set, but somehow the words wouldn't stop leaving her mouth. "Don't you find that rather odd? I mean, coincidence is altogether much too convenient. I guess what I'm trying to say is that fate has something planned for you. Something great. . .but you have to wait for it. You can't fight for something that doesn't belong to you."

Zabuli furrowed her brow strangely at Lydia, as if she were somewhat impressed with what she said, but she wasn't convinced. At this point, Lydia was only trying to come up with anything she could say to stall Zabuli so she could think of a plan to get her and Mr. Miller out of this mess.

"And—you know—magic probably complicates things a bit. I'm sure you'd probably know that, but, well, wouldn't you think it would—I don't know—maybe—make everything a little less real?" Lydia's eyes flicked around the room to see if there was something that could help her. "You know, with the whole golden dust thing I'm sure you'll only get bored of it all. Getting *everything* you want? It gets bland after a while. I mean, I get bored of being around my best friend after only a day. Imagine a whole *decade* of the same thing over and over and over again." The two watched her with strange expressions. Mr. Miller tried to motion for her to stop, but she paid him no heed. She just needed a bit more time. "I suppose you probably know all of this already, Ms. Candy, but I did indeed have a row with Cedric. You know why? Because of *love*. Love is the trickiest of things on this earth. *Far* trickier than magic. Funnily enough though, either thing can kill you." She chuckled to herself, but suddenly her eyes noticed a bunch of bottles lining a shelf about a meter away from her. A variety of dusts and liquids filled the glass: pink powder, blue goo, strange leaves, but one bottle filled with black dust and a label that read *Necare* stood out to her.

"Are you finished yet?" Zabuli half-groaned. "I might have to take you out first." She held the dust in her direction, to which Mr. Miller exclaimed "no!" Lydia, though terrified, took her chance.

She held her hands up and pretended to back away from Zabuli, but only inched closer to the shelf holding the powder until it was right within her reach.

"You know," Lydia thought out loud in a mocking sort of way, "For someone who's been waiting so long for this opportunity, you're taking an awfully long time to actually do it."

Mr. Miller's eyes grew wide as he shook his head furiously at Lydia. She made a subtle gesture back to imply that she knew what she was doing.

Zabuli scoffed. "Well, aren't you a great know-it-all! You seem to think you know so much about my intent, don't you?"

"Actually, I do." Lydia said with her nose in the air. "You're not going to lay a *finger* on him."

"And why is that?"

Lydia shifted uncomfortably. "Because you'll have to kill *me* first."

Zabuli laughed wildly. Mr. Miller motioned for Lydia to shut it again, but she disregarded him and kept her brave facade in the face of a mocking witch. "You think I wouldn't?"

"I can't imagine that would look very good on your part, you know," Lydia said with a smart-aleck tone. "Ms. Candy, killing the only daughter of the Maylers, the family everyone in town knows and loves?"

"You think I'm stupid, Lydia?" Ms. Candy scoffed. "I could make you disappear in an instant and *no one* would be the wiser."

"Then do it."

It fell deadly silent.

Mr. Miller's breath caught in his throat as Zabuli glanced at him, then back to Lydia.

"You're willing to *die* for this man?"

"Yes." Lydia swallowed hard. "I am."

"*Vincent Miller*? You're willing to sacrifice your life for *Vincent Miller*?"

Lydia's eye shot to the grey powder on the shelf.

So close...

Zabuli raised an eyebrow as if that might elicit a response any faster. With one last smile to Mr. Miller (in the event that this plan went horribly wrong), Lydia stared Zabuli straight in the eye and smiled.

"Actually," she said, whipping around to grab the small gray vial—"It's Hugo."

She reached her arm back and chucked the vial right at Zabuli's feet. Throwing herself under a desk and praying it didn't hit Mr. Miller, she covered herself and peeked over to watch if her plan succeeded.

The witch shrieked and flailed about as her body fell to dust. Mr. Miller watched in horror and cringed at the sight. Zabuli, though turning to dust, tried to throw herself to grab Lydia, but she only made it one step until her legs crumpled beneath her. With one last evil look, she ceased her crying and dissolved into a puff of smoke. All that remained where she stood was a pile of black dust and wilted roses blooming from the ashes.

Lydia climbed to her feet shakily, out of breath and in shock from the instance that just occurred. Her eyes remained fixated on the remains of a woman she had known her whole life, but never really knew in the first place. Then, she looked to the man she had only just met, but knew better than anyone else in the world.

Grabbing a silver knife that was jammed into the desk, Lydia yanked it out and cut the ropes from Mr. Miller's hands and feet. He grimaced, rubbing the irritated skin. He closed his eyes and took in a deep breath, saying nothing to Lydia who was watching him closely.

"Don't say anything," she said when he started to speak. "It's my fault this whole mess happened in the first place."

"It would've happened no matter what you had done," he replied. Lydia shook her head no, but Mr. Miller objected. "What's meant to happen will happen. Just like you said." Lydia paused, but kept her head down. "Zabuli would've gotten to me one way or another, and I must say I am very grateful it happened like this." He bent down and crinkled one of the withered flowers in his hands. "And I'm incredibly grateful to have the brightest friends in the world."

Lydia half smiled, then glanced back down to the pile of ash on the floor. "It's over so quickly, isn't it? After so long of waiting for this one moment, it's just. . .finished."

He shrugged and stood back to his feet, wandering over to a table with open books of spells and potions. "That's the funny thing about time. It slows when it shouldn't, and the moment you wish it would stop, it speeds up."

Then, as usual, Lydia could not contain the burning thought within her. "About Laurie. . ." He tensed up and kept his back towards her. "I'm really, really sorry."

He remained still, then sniffed and ran his hand through his hair. "Me, too." He turned and looked at her. "I think you two would've been dear friends."

She chuckled. "Dear friends? Much like you and—" Bastien! She had nearly forgotten! "Bastien! He's here! He's trapped behind bars!" Lydia gasped. Mr. Miller became very alert at once.

"Take me to him."

* * *

They hurried down the spiraling stairs and into the dark hallways of the castle. It took a bit of navigating to figure out her way back, but Lydia managed to lead Mr. Miller to the cold cell where Bastien and Pippin waited anxiously. Pippin was hanging onto the rails of Bastien's cell, trying to nudge them open, but doing no good.

"Bastien!" Lydia exclaimed, falling to her knees and hanging onto the bars to look.

"I don't know what happened, he just collapsed," Pippin cried.

Bastien lay on the floor facing away from them as if he had been knocked unconscious. Mr. Miller grabbed one of the steel torches from the wall and knocked the lock open. He went to grab Bastien's arms to drag him out, but then Bastien twitched. Mr. Miller's breath caught in his throat. Bastien moved again, then roused awake.

He groaned in pain. "Oh, my head. . ."

Pulling himself up unto his hands, he put a hand on his head to try and stop the aching, but something felt different. Something in the way he moved, and his voice, Lydia thought.

When Bastien's hand ran through his hair, he froze. Then, he touched it again. Then again. His breathing caught up. He examined his hand closely and traced the edges of each finger and wrinkle. When he managed to climb to his feet, he patted himself down and laughed.

"I'm. . ." Bastien slowly turned around and at last they could see his face.

His hair fell past his ears, and though his skin was pale like milk, his cheeks were pink and flushed. When he smiled, the room lit up like a lantern, even though it was dark and upsetting in the stone cell. He traced his face in disbelief.

"I'm Bastien again."

Lydia and Mr. Miller looked at other.

"I'm Bastien again!"

Mr. Miller laughed then brought his friend close and tight. Bastien's eyes turned red. He held him at arm's length and smiled brightly, with perfectly white teeth and the kindest eyes Lydia had ever seen.

"It's good to see you again," Mr. Miller said.

"Isn't it?"

Pippin breathed a sigh of relief that Bastien was not, in fact, dead, but very much alive. More alive than ever. Bastien crouched down to a wide-eyed Pippin and shook his hand.

"How about a do-over?"

Pippin croaked. "You look different."

"I should hope so." He took his time extending his legs and arms, making sure he felt every muscle move and every breath enter his lungs.

"How do you feel?" Lydia stepped closer.

He chuckled. "Never better."

Bastien then focused back to Mr. Miller, as if he had just realized something he had long forgotten. When he caught Mr. Miller's eye, it was clear they were both thinking the same thing.

"I can go back now," Bastien said. "Can't I?"

Mr. Miller nodded. His friend laughed with joy and grabbed Pippin to throw him up in the air. Pippin shrieked, then chuckled nervously when he was set back down. Lydia figure he was still shaken from the dragonfly and from watching Bastien's supposed death. No matter, she thought, it was all over with.

After a while of retracing steps and getting lost multiple times, the four managed to find their way out of the castle. The second they stepped out, the stone and marble crumpled to smoke and gray shimmering dust. Mr. Miller smiled and wiped his hands of any debris.

"At last the witch has left us."

15

And, just as quickly as everything first happened, everything changed once more. How strange, Lydia thought, that it took so much to accomplish a moment that ended in a mere second.

Mr. Miller took Lydia's dragonfly and opened it on the ground. He was a much better pilot than Lydia, something of which she and Pippin were very grateful for. The sky turned blue and sunny the longer they traveled the great scale of the earth. Bastien held his arms out and let the wind blow his hair back from his face.

The only thing in him that left was a curse. He still retained that dearest dramatic flair and joy within him. Every so often, Mr. Miller would glance back at his grand smile and laugh. Their whole friendship was beautiful, Lydia thought, and though she *was* very happy for the two of them, seeing their friendship blossom caused an aching in her heart. She really *did* miss Cedric, even if she was still mad at him.

The dragonfly passed through a giant stone arch where the two sides of the wall had completely different settings. Where they were now, it was bright and midday, but when they passed through to the other side, the sun was only just rising and the forest had no whimsy and charm.

"Brightmeadow at last," Bastien said.

When they walked back into the shop, a note awaited them on the table with pretty handwriting:

Au revoir, my friends. Come see me on the stage.
Antoinette Bellefeuille

"I'm going to miss her," Bastien chuckled. "Fiery, but a dear friend."

He nodded in response, then took the letter and tacked it onto the side of the drawers for everyone to see. Though sad Antoinette left so soon, Lydia understood. She would miss Antoinette. She was nice company to have around, but Lydia had no doubt Antoinette would find deep joy in the life she fairly regained.

A loud, rolling noise cut through the air. Mr. Miller pulled out a familiar door from the corner behind a curtain. He nodded his head for Pippin to come closer. Mr. Miller's key fit into the doorway, and the wonderful land of Carmen opened in all of its spectacular glory. Pippin laughed with joy and hurried through, waving to all the creatures passing by with loads of enthusiasm. Lydia and the others followed him through. She had walked these grassy hills before, but nothing could ever prepare her for the feeling when she entered. It was just as it was the first time she walked through to this magical land: like she had come up from water and taken a deep breath, or when she walked into a cold room after being in the heat all day. It reminded her of a warm drink on a snowy evening, or sleep after a tiring day. She leaned down and ran her hand along the wavy grass that flowed gently in the sweet breeze.

Although Pippin seemed all too relieved to be home, Lydia could tell something troubled him. They all walked a little ways together one last time, taking in the final memories. Pippin led them down a path by the side of the pub which led to a cute little neighborhood with giant mushroom houses. He pointed out one towards the center that had a quaint white fence and pretty flowers.

Bastien chuckled lightly to himself. "You know, Pippin, I'm actually going to miss you."

He perked up. "Really?"

"Really." He leaned down beside him. "You have a beautiful heart. Don't ever lose it."

Mr. Miller gave Pippin a silver pin with a rose pierced by a sword. "For excellent valor and bravery in the face of fear," he said. He clipped it onto his vest. Pippin smiled brightly. Then, the moment he dreaded most began.

Lydia tilted her head and smiled at the sweet little creature, who stared back up at her just as dreamily as he did the first time he saw her.

"I don't want you to go, Lydia." He frowned. "I don't think I'll ever find someone as kind as you again."

She chuckled and leaned down beside him. "That's not true, Pippin. Besides, one day you're going to meet a very lovely lady, and she's going to love you more than anyone else in the world."

"But what if I never meet her?"

"I know you will, Pippin."

"How?"

She tapped the pin on his vest. "Because you always find people exactly when they need to be found. That's your magic, remember?"

He smiled, then wrapped his arms around Lydia. Taken by surprise, she patted his back gently.

"Here. Take this." Lydia took one of the silver rings on her finger and handed it to him. "Just so you never forget us."

"I couldn't even if I tried." He sniffled lightly. "One day, I hope we find each other once more."

"I have no doubt in my mind that we will."

16

Bastien ran around the store in a frenzy, throwing an assortment of things in his large, leather suitcase. Mr. Miller helped him sort it out and when neither was looking, Lydia would take things back out of the case, fold them, then put them back in.

Bastien mumbled frantically under his breath. "And all of my bowties, where are they. . .and the jacket, don't forget the others. . ."

At last, he had everything together. He stood proudly and sighed, placing this hands on his hips and rubbing his forehead.

"Sweat! I had forgotten what that felt like." He rubbed his head again, then once more, then one more time for good measure.

"Aren't you forgetting something?" Mr. Miller raised an eyebrow.

Bastien thought to himself for a moment, then rummaged through the case again. "I don't think—oh! Oh, I have!" He hurried to the back of the store, then reemerged holding a violin case. "How could I possibly forget Wolfgang? Dear friend, I am *so* sorry."

Mr. Miller pushed the Carmen door back into a corner, then pushed aside a dark, velvet curtain that Lydia hadn't noticed before. He rolled mahogany door into view. Lydia tilted her head curiously as Mr. Miller wiped away the dust on the handle. Bastien's breath caught in his throat. Slowly, he approached it in deep silence and contemplation. He put his hand upon it, tracing every detail with his finger and running his palm along the edge.

"You still have the door?" Bastien's face lit up.

"Of course I do," Mr. Miller replied. "I would never rid of it."

Mr. Miller pulled the necklace from his neck and sorted through his keys, then picked a golden one shaped like a violin. He unlocked the door and pushed it open.

"Welcome home, Bastien."

Beneath a lavender sky, people in posh, victorian clothing swayed to and fro across a cobblestone street. A horse and buggy galloped through the crowd with a very important looking couple lounging in the carriage. Brilliantly structured buildings stretched down the street with light blue smoke puffing from the chimneys. Old shop windows advertised custom clothing and homemade baked goods. The smell of sweet bread and honey overcame the powerful fumes of city life. A group of musicians played an up-beat tune on stringed instruments by the corner of two shops. In the distance, a grand cathedral's bells rang out eight times. The sky flowed with lovely lavender colors and golden, pink clouds.

"I can't believe I'm here," Bastien whispered. "I never thought I'd be able to see any of this again."

"Capriccioso hasn't changed a bit," Mr. Miller said. "But I know for a fact it will only be better with you in it."

After they all stepped through the door, Lydia looked back and saw that their entrance was attached to a shop labeled:

Mr. Miller's Shop of Antiques and Antiquities

"So, is there anywhere in particular that you would like to go?" Mr. Miller asked, but he said it in such a way it was obvious that he already knew what the answer was. Bastien nodded.

He led them down the stone street for a few blocks, then turned into a wider road with an iron fence. They passed into an eccentric neighborhood, where Lydia had no doubt the richest of the community lived. It was like the Dahlia Road of Capriccioso, where the ladies always looked lovely and the gentleman always held the door.

"I didn't know you lived in such a wonderfully kept place," Lydia marveled. "Mrs. Fisher would be very jealous."

Bastien laughed and shook his head. "*Me?* No, of course not. I live on the other side of town. I'm here to see someone else."

"So you *don't* live so grandly?"

"I play violin for a living, Lydia," he said. "I live in a closet."

Flowers lined the sides of the streets up to a grand white mansion with black shutters and ivy growing up the sides of the chimney. The yard had a large, black-iron fence with a stone road and a grey fountain in the middle of a round-a-bout. With dumb luck, the gate was partially open, just enough for Bastien to open it all the way. He led them to the side of the house and stood beneath a window with lace curtains.

"What are we doing here?" Lydia murmured to Mr. Miller, but he said nothing and motioned for her to stand back and watch.

Bastien took Wolfgang from his case and tuned the strings, plucking each one carefully. He rosined his bow, sending small puffs of dust flying from the sides. Lydia sensed his nerves and could hear his heart beating from where she stood. He hesitated, as if to rethink his choices, then leveled the bow to his chin and played a sweet, solemn tune.

For a moment, nothing happened. Bastien continued playing, occasionally glancing up to the window nervously. He stopped, flustered, then breathed heavily and continued on. The curtains ruffled behind the window and Lydia noticed the eyes of a young lady peek out from between them. Bastien played louder, then caught her eye. By the look on his face, his heart stopped when he saw her.

The young lady ran from the window in a hurry, but Bastien didn't stop playing. Instead, a sly smile pulled at his lips as he tune carried on. The sound of a door flying open rang in the air and next thing she knew, the young lady from the window was running towards Bastien with teary eyes and long, red, curly hair flying behind her. Bastien barely had time to sit Wolfgang back into his case before the lady grabbed him and threw her arms around him. Bastien held her close and sunk his head into the crook of her shoulder. He picked her up and spun her around in the air. She laughed and brought him close once more.

"I thought I'd never see you again," she spoke through falling tears. "Bastien, what took you so long?"

"You have them to thank." Bastien brought his eyes to Lydia and Mr. Miller. All of a sudden, a thousand memories came back to her. She couldn't help but tear up at her many thoughts and at the shining face before her that made her realize life was only what you made of it. The lady came toward an unprepared Lydia and grabbed her tightly. Though Lydia could hardly breathe, she let it happen, knowing that it probably meant the world to her.

"I will never be able to thank you enough." She tucked Lydia's hair behind her ear. "Your heart is woven from kindness."

Lydia smiled bashfully. "Thank you, ma'am. Bastien truly is one of a kind. You chose well."

Her eyes moved to Mr. Miller, who fiddled with hands anxiously. "Oh, Hugo, it's wonderful to see you again." She hugged him tightly. "I've missed you."

"And I, you, Miss Beatrice."

She turned back to Bastien and grabbed his hands gently. "You came back for me? Even after all this time has passed?"

Bastien moved her hair away from her face. "You waited all these years for me." He squeezed her hands delicately. "That is the grandest love I can ever imagine."

Mr. Miller smiled sadly, a smile of which only Lydia took notice of. Bastien had never looked so truly whole, and it baffled Lydia to see him in his most human form. Beatrice tucked his hair behind his ear and turned back over to Mr. Miller and Lydia.

"Beatrice, it was great seeing you again," he said. "Unfortunately, I must make my way back home. I have some important duties to attend." Mr. Miller bowed to acknowledge Beatrice one last time, then began to move towards the road, but Bastien didn't move. He only stood transfixed at the beauty in front of him and the feeling of flesh and blood. Bastien's eyes flicked to Beatrice, then to Mr. Miller, who was beginning to try to accept what would happen next.

Mr. Miller pursed his lips and watched his friend, whom he had known for the best parts of his life, grow up more in a few minutes than he had in the past thirty years. His eyes grew red and watery, the first time Lydia had seen Bastien cry that truly mattered.

"I think I'm going to stay." Bastien said these words with hopefully, but could not deny the shaky manner in which he spoke. Mr. Miller nodded to hide the sadness in his voice.

"I know."

And in a moment of fleeting silence, which seemed to last an eternity between them, Mr. Miller nodded one last goodbye and motioned for Lydia to follow him back to the door. There was so much Lydia wanted to say—she wanted to tell Mr. Miller to say something, *anything*. The very person who saved Mr. Miller on multiple occasions was leaving, and all he was going to do was wave goodbye?

Mr. Miller paused at the gate, then shook his head to himself and started through, when suddenly Bastien's voice cut through the solemn moment.

"Wait!"

Mr. Miller turned around to see Bastien hurrying towards him, then wrapping his arms around him tightly. Mr. Miller appeared taken aback, but gave in. Lydia knew in an instant that was exactly what he needed. A true goodbye and a final salute to a friendship that changed the lives of two people who only wanted something of which they indeed finally found. Just when Lydia thought they might pull away, they didn't. It was a sudden reminder to her about how lonely she used to be. Before all *this:* Before Mr. Miller, Bastien, Antoinette, and Pippin. And, even though she had only known them for a short time, she felt as if she had known them her whole life. Bastien especially, for it was he himself that made Lydia believe there was more to everything. She gave him his life back, and he gave her life in return.

Mr. Miller held Bastien at an arm's length and smiled. "I'm going to miss you, old friend."

"Not nearly as much as I shall miss you."

He focused to Lydia, then pulled her in for a warm embrace. The plastic replaced itself with flesh, blood, and the beating heart Bastien always carried with him: a heart of wonder. "Lydia Mayler. I owe everything to you."

"And I, you."

Bastien kissed her forehead lightly and hugged her once more.

"Come visit sometime, alright?" Lydia asked.

"Of course. You won't be able to keep me away."

As she walked away, she didn't let go of his hand until the very last second.

Mr. Miller smiled and bowed his head slightly, then led Lydia back down the road. As hard as he tried to hide it, he couldn't conceal his red eyes and flushed cheeks from the very observant Lydia.

When they reached the end of the street, he turned around and watched Bastien laugh and twirl Beatrice around in the air. He smiled and shook his head sadly.

"I'm going to miss that one."

Lydia nodded. She knew it best not to reply, but to just let him speak his thoughts.

He watched Bastien, laughing and smiling with the one he had loved for so long. He brushed the curls away from her face and kissed her forehead. Mr. Miller smiled. "So long, old friend. I wish you the truest of happiness." With one last wave goodbye, he turned his head and made his way back down the joyful streets of Capriccioso.

17

Night had fallen in Brightmeadow. Lydia knew she was unable to return home. She figured she would spend another night asleep in the shop chair, which she didn't really mind, but she worried for the coming days. She couldn't stay here *forever.* Mr. Miller left her a blanket and told her to stay as long as she'd like, but there was another question nagging her.

"You're going to leave, too," she said as he went to leave the room. "Aren't you?"

He stopped for a moment, then turned back to face Lydia. "I think so."

She nodded, revealing no sign of the sadness she felt. "Better get some rest, then?"

He half-chuckled. "Good night."

And then he left.

It was suddenly all too quiet for Lydia. Usually, the shop was filled with some kind of noise: arguing, laughing, and other conversations that would be considered strange to any rational person. There were no more violins or harps, no more shouting. . .

Only quiet.

Lydia re-read Antoinette's letter over and over again. She missed them all already. And, even though he wasn't gone yet, Lydia also missed Mr. Miller.

She didn't mean to, but she fell asleep as she recounted every second of the memories she would give anything to relive. Her dreams were fantastical and grand, yet even in her greatest imagination, she couldn't escape the sorrow of her friends leaving. As she awoke to the clear dawn of morning, the figures in her dreams waved their goodbyes and disappeared in a haze of sunlight.

She wiped the grogginess from her eyes and yawned. Mr. Miller wasn't in sight. Today was a new day, which was both frightening and exciting to Lydia. As she had learned, so much can happen in a single day.

She thought it rather wonderful.

The sun shone bright along Dandelion Lane, and when she turned on Magnolia, she made sure to not get too close to her mother's shop. Instead, she sat on the black iron fence in the quiet of morning and watched a few dozen people trickle by. The church bells rang six times and, much to her surprise, the whistle of the trolley rang in her ears. The cart came rolling down the street holding a sweet couple and the trolley driver. Lydia chuckled and tilted her head as she watched it pass by the station.

At this moment, she wished for nothing more than to speak to Cedric, but she knew it was a silly thing to think. He had his mind made up, and he made his decision. Her heart still hung miserably, but she did her best to try and dismiss it. There were other things to worry about.

And, though she said she wouldn't, Lydia couldn't help but think about the flower shop. She would never sit behind that dreaded counter again and groan about the customers, or sit and laugh with Cedric about the most unimportant of things. Honestly, she didn't really know what she would do now that everyone was gone.

Suddenly, she remembered what Mr. Miller had said the night before.

Before Lydia returned back to the shop, she passed by her old home and slipped a letter inside of the empty mailbox.

***

When Lydia returned to the shop, Mr. Miller stood outside with a leather bag and a look of nostalgia on his face as he gazed up at the green sign. She approached him quietly, but she could tell he knew she was there.

"I did this all for her," he said to himself. "And she never even got to see it."

Lydia tilted her head. "Laurie?"

He nodded, then stayed quiet for a moment. He glanced down at his hand and motioned toward the ring on his right hand. "Do you remember asking me if this place was even a shop because I never sold anything?"

"I do."

He smiled lightly. "It was all of her things. All those notes and scraps and strange items—I just—couldn't bring myself to part with it all."

Lydia's heart squeezed. It struck her as terribly sad, that someone who had lost so much in his life still had so much hope and joy in a world that just kept taking. She admired him a lot for this. Bitterness had not touched his heart, which is something that couldn't be said for most people.

"What changed your mind?" Lydia asked.

"You."

"Me?" Her voice wavered. "Why?"

He smiled. "You remind me a lot of her."

"Who? Antoinette?"

"No." He shook his head. "Laurie." Lydia's breath caught in her throat. Perhaps that's why Mr. Miller treated her as one of his own all this time. He saw her as family, the one he lost far too soon. "She didn't make it long, but. . ." He trailed off for a moment. "She was just like you. Kind. . .and brave."

Lydia could not think of anything to say. "I'm sorry."

He nodded, but it was clear he had something else on his mind. "Lydia, I need you to promise me something." She tilted her head. "Never take your days for granted. Each second is more precious than a pound of gold. I used to not understand, but then—then I lost everyone in this world I cared about." He paused. "So promise me that until your dying day, you'll appreciate every minute of your life, even the ones you wish would be over."

"I promise," she said quietly. "Though I know I have no control over the seconds I have been granted."

He agreed and fiddled with the ring on his hand. "There's nothing you can do about the days you have except be glad you have them."

Lydia watched the sign sway in the wind and the expression in his eyes change. There was a certain hope for the future, yet an evident fear hid itself within that spirit of fire, coursing through his veins with excitement and wonder. He was such a strange person. Anyone else in his position would likely have given up on a life worth living, but there he stood, ready to try again.

She wondered how many times he had tried again. She figured the stories he could tell were beyond this world, but she understood his new hesitation to leave such a polite and humble place.

Lydia admired him greatly. There he stood after losing his whole world, then finding it in his two best friends who were then cursed. And, when the curse was finally broken, they forged their own lives from the fire that had burnt them out. Mr. Miller was happy for them of course, but Lydia knew better than to assume he wasn't heartbroken at the loss of his friends. She understood what it felt like though, as she currently found herself in the middle of the same situation.

"Well," she began, "If you ever need a break from the world, Brightmeadow will always be here."

Mr. Miller chuckled to himself and began to reply, but as soon as he did, Lydia noticed a familiar figure approaching her with a nervous expression. Lydia held her hand up apologetically. "One moment, please."

Cedric walked towards her with his head down in a shameful way. Although Lydia *was* mad at him, she didn't think he should look so ashamed. He glanced at her, then back down, and handed her a small box with a blue ribbon on it.

"I was going to get you a flower, but I figured that would be inappropriate since your mother owns a flower shop."

"Good choice," Lydia half-chuckled. She opened the box and pulled out a silver key. "What's this?"

He took a deep breath. "When you told me no, I realized that was the first time in my life I ever really felt. . .*sad*. I didn't understand it, and I didn't understand what to do, and so I made mistakes. And I'm sorry." Lydia nodded along as he continued with his story. "My parents still expect me to get married, even if it's not with you. I understand that, and I respect your decision."

"Thank you," Lydia quickly interjected in his speech.

Cedric smiled half-heartedly, then sighed. "So that means in the coming year I am expected to wed Caroline Arden." Lydia's stomach dropped at the sound of this news. So *that's* why they had been spending so much time together, and *that's* why he was so weird about the whole thing. And, though it was a horrible thought, she couldn't help but note how similar her and Caroline were in appearance. With that said, all she truly wanted was for Cedric to be happy, but she could tell this choice was not of his own free will. As much as he tried to play it off, Lydia could see through it all. "*That* is a key to our new home. I was hoping that—you know—any time you would like, you would come and visit us."

Lydia smiled. "I would love to."

"Really?" Cedric's eyes flicked up hopefully.

"Of course."

He breathed a sigh of relief. "Perhaps. . .perhaps it won't be so bad, then."

Lydia scrunched her lips to the side. "I hope you two find happiness." She met his eyes. "*True* happiness."

"Is there such a thing?"

Lydia looked back at the shop, its green sign swaying with each blow of wind.

"I think so."

Cedric glanced down at his feet. "How lucky are those who find such true things with no compromises."

She smiled. It was an old smile, like she called upon some grand past memory to express it with. The same smile when she first met Cedric; the same smile when they spent every lunch together; the same smile when she climbed all the way up that tree that happened to change her life forever.

"How lucky, indeed."

Then, out of seemingly nowhere, Mrs. Fisher appeared and cut their moment right in two. Lydia couldn't help but feel the slightest bit guilty since she *did* accuse this innocent woman of being a witch, but the guilt promptly faded when the lady opened her mouth. "Lydia, how good to see you! Cedric, you've gotten taller."

"You saw me last week."

"I saw that dress you made on display in your mother's shop, Lydia. It's quite impressive."

"She put it on display?" She must have searched her room after she disappeared, Lydia thought. The dress wasn't hard to find, it was only under her bed. But her mother put it on *display*? Lydia's heart fluttered with excitement, then weighed heavy with guilt and sadness.

"She sure did. Which reminds me—" Mrs. Fisher dug around in her purse and handed Lydia a golden slip of paper with shiny trim and fancy lettering:

Eleanor Fisher cordially invites you to her spring celebration ball. Friday night, eight o'clock. Please come in your finest attire.

"I was hoping you'd wear it to the ball next Friday." Mrs. Fisher popped a candy in her mouth. "I would absolutely love for you to show it off to everyone. What do you say?"

Lydia laughed with joy. At last! She had done it. She couldn't think of anything to say. For so long, she wanted to be able to show off her gift at the perfect ball with the perfect people. When she glanced back up at Mrs. Fisher's expectant face though, something in her changed. It was as if it were a goal she somehow already accomplished, and suddenly it didn't feel so important at all.

"Thank you, Mrs. Fisher. That sounds lovely. But I'm afraid I have my own duties I must attend to."

She appeared taken aback. Dabbling at the perspiration on her forehead with a handkerchief, she gave one last smile to Lydia and Cedric. "Well, alright then. If you change your mind you know where to find me. Good afternoon to you both." With a chipper pep in her step, she fluttered away in a cloud of perfume and money.

Cedric chuckled lightly. "I don't think she's ever been told 'no' before."

"She'll get over it."

A silence settled between them, but it said more than words ever could.

"So. . .I'll see you around, then?"

Lydia shrugged. "Maybe. Maybe not. If you don't, you know where I'll be."

He nodded. "I sure do." Tipping his hat, he began to walk down the quiet street. "Cheers for now, Miss Mayler."

"Cheers!"

Mr. Miller observed from under the sign with a pleased smile. He reminded Lydia of how much she had grown up in such a short time. Soon, she would grow old and only have her memories.

She was grateful that she could now look back on them with joy.

"So," she said, "I suppose this is our goodbye."

Mr. Miller averted his eyes over the blue horizon. "I suppose it is."

Lydia pursed her lips. "Am I ever going to see you again?"

His brow furrowed in the bright sun. "I'd count on it."

He dug into his pocket and handed her a gold coin, just like he did twice before. Lydia smiled and ran her finger along the edge of it, suddenly feeling a deep sense of nostalgia. At last, she felt she had friends that understood her, and now they were all gone. She was so happy for all of them, but all at once she felt lonely again. "There's something else I want you to have."

"Oh?"

Mr. Miller reached around his neck and took off the chain holding the keys and charms. With one last sigh full of the richest memories, he presented it to a baffled Lydia.

"The shop. And all that goes with it."

"Oh, no, I really couldn't. That's all too much," she said. He trusted her with his own shop? The very thing that kept him going for all those years?

"I can think of no one braver, wiser, or more intelligent to inherit my life of the past. If it weren't for you, we'd all be goners. Lydia Mayler, it would be my highest honor for you to become the owner."

Lydia smiled and took the chain from him, placing it around her neck carefully. A sudden flurry of a thousand feelings filled her at once.

"I'm not sure how I could ever thank you," she said.

"You already have."

Lydia contemplated whether or not to say what she was thinking, but gave in. "You know. . .you can say it all you want, but you're the furthest thing from a lousy wizard."

He chuckled and tilted his head to the side. "There was always more to it than just being a wizard. I realize that now."

She nodded, but didn't quite understand what he meant. "How do you know it's all okay in the end? All this, I mean." She motioned back to the shop.

"Because you're here." He smiled. "And that's never going to change."

Lydia shrugged. "Someday, maybe. Life just moves too quickly to be able to really know what you want."

"Yes, Lydia, life is fleeting," he said, "But isn't that rather the point?"

She ran her hand over the charms and keys on the necklace. Each was labeled in tiny, engraved writing. Though they were worn and rusted around the edges, Lydia had never felt so new.

"So what now?" She glanced up at him. "Where do you think you'll go next?"

He sighed and gazed behind her for a moment. "I intend to find where the earth meets the sky." Lydia only watched him as he struggled to speak his next words. He never lied, but she found that the truth was often more frightening than a thought.

"And?"

He ran his hand through his hair and scoffed, as if to acknowledge how well she knew him. "And chase the feeling I once was so frightened to be content with."

"Maybe fall in love?"

He pursed his lips and shrugged. "I suppose if my heart allows it."

"The heart doesn't allow most anything," Lydia said with a furrowed brow. "It goes to where we least want it to."

He smiled and thought about her words carefully, taking one last breath of fresh air as he gathered up his things. He reach his hand out in front of him.

"Until next time."

She shook his hand tightly. "Until next time, Hugo."

He chuckled lightly. "Hugo?"

"Of course. We're friends right?"

"Yes." He grinned. "Yes we are." He pulled the dragonfly from his pocket and placed it on the ground. The wings spread open and the all too familiar plane popped into view. Mr. Miller stepped aboard, glancing back at Lydia.

"Don't ever forget me."

"*Forget* you?" She shook her head. "Impossible."

Then, next thing she knew, Hugo disappeared with a glimmer of dust, and all she could see was a buzzing dragonfly circling around her head.

"Oh, just go! And be careful!" Lydia giggled. With one last zip, it flew up into the wonderful sky. "So long!"

And in an instant, he was gone, and Lydia was alone. But not really. Hugo wasn't *really* gone, and Lydia wasn't *really* alone. Their hearts still resided in the dusty old shelves of that old shop, beating inside of the trinkets and memories held within it. Lydia looked up at the green sign swaying in the wind, recalling the very first time she laid her eyes on it. Suddenly, the name just didn't feel so right anymore.

So, with the help of a ladder and a few handy tools, Lydia took down the sign and began her work, painting and perfecting every detail. When the sun was highest in the sky the next day, she placed it right back on the hangers for all of Dandelion Lane to see; for all of Dandelion Lane to admire; for all of Dandelion Lane to hope for.

How funny.

She once believed she would never run a shop here, for fear of missing out on adventure. But here she is, and the only reason she could adventure was *because* of this old shop. And, perhaps one day, a young, bored girl would wander inside in search of an adventure, to which Lydia would give her the greatest dreams she could. For this store was so much more than just a building with a few antiques. It was every dream Lydia wished for, and every wonder she had hoped for. With one last smile to the new sign hanging in the wind, Lydia held the key to her heart and rung the bell on the door to her new store:

Miss Mayler's Shop of Curious Antiquities

Epilogue

    To Lydia, it appeared time had a nasty habit of never stopping. The years seemed to churn on and on after the departure of Hugo. Every so often, she would receive a magical little postcard with moving pictures of him traveling around the globe. Lydia herself had been very busy traveling far and wide as well, but it brought her a grand amount of joy to see the happiness of her friend who deserved it more than anyone.

    After a day visit to Capriccioso, Lydia caught word of a show happening in the city of Paris. The past few weeks had proved themselves rather boring, so she decided to travel to the lovely city for a day of adventure.

    The skies greeted her with a delicate warmth and a chill in the air. The smell of bakeries and coffee tickled her nose as the streets crowded with people of all kinds: artists, lovers, and the loners, the three sorts of people who made the world of any worth.

She managed to snag a ticket to the show (with very good seating!) from a man who was selling his. Unfortunately, he had to leave town that day and the ticket did him no good, so Lydia bought it for a third of the price. On the way to the theatre, she purchased a croissant from a nearby bakery with a man who seemed very old, yet had the youth and joy of someone much younger. She tipped him generously.

The theatre smelled of velvet and old paper, a smell of which Lydia loved dearly. Ladies in long, expensive coats and golden gloves settled in with men in nice suits and hats. The crowd mumbled and whispered amongst themselves in the red seats until the lights dimmed. At once, a silence fell over the audience.

The curtains opened and the orchestra began to play a soft, delicate tune beginning with a single violin. When the lights cast down on the wooden stage, a single dancer lifted her head and just so happened to directly meet eyes with Lydia.

She smiled brightly, and Lydia smiled right back.

Acknowledgements

To my family, for being the first to read this and being the best supporters I could ask for. I love you all.

To Katie Middlecoff, for being the best editor I could ask for.

To the coffee shop in Collierville, for occasionally giving me ventis instead of grandes when you all saw that I was writing.

To all of my dear friends who have been so supportive of me in this journey.

Made in the USA
Monee, IL
19 October 2021